Elsie and
Her Loved Ones

The Original Elsie Classics

Elsie and Her Loved Ones

Book Twenty-Seven of
The Original Elsie Classics

Martha Finley

CUMBERLAND HOUSE
NASHVILLE, TENNESSEE

Elsie and Her Loved Ones
by Martha Finley

Any unique characteristics of this edition:
Copyright © 2001 by Cumberland House Publishing, Inc.

Published by Cumberland House Publishing, Inc.,
431 Harding Industrial Drive, Nashville, Tennessee 37211.

Cover design by Bruce Gore, Gore Studios, Inc.
Photography by Dean Dixon Photography
Hair and Makeup by Calene Rader
Text design by Heather Armstrong

Printed in the United States of America
1 2 3 4 5 6 7 8 — 05 04 03 02 01

CHAPTER FIRST

IT WAS A LOVELY spring day at Viamede, where Mrs. Travilla—or Grandma Elsie, as some of her young friends called her—was seated under the orange trees on the flower-bespangled lawn with her father and his wife, Mr. Ronald Lilburn and his wife, Annis, her children, and some of the more distant relatives and friends gathered about her. Some others were wandering about at some little distance on the same beautiful lawn.

"What a beautiful place this is!" exclaimed Zoe, breaking a pause in the conversation.

"Yes," said her husband, "but I am thinking it is probably about time we returned to our more northern homes."

"I think it is," said his grandfather, Mr. Dinsmore.

"I, also. I feel as if I had been neglecting my business shamefully," sighed Chester.

At that, Dr. Harold shook his head smilingly. "Don't let conscience reproach you, Chester, for what has probably saved you from invalidism and perhaps prolonged your life for years."

"Well, cousin doctor, you will surely have to admit that I am well enough to go back to work now?" laughed Chester.

"Perhaps, but wait a little till you hear a plan I have to propose. Mother," he went on, turning to her, "I met a gentleman yesterday who has just returned from California, which he pronounces the loveliest, most salubrious section of our country. What he had to say of its climate and scenery has aroused in me a strange desire to visit it, taking you all with me, especially those of our party who are my patients."

"Hardly at this time of year, though, I suppose, Harold," she replied, giving him a look of loving appreciation. "It would seem wiser to move in a more northerly direction before the summer heats come on."

"Well, mother, this gentleman says the summers there are really more enjoyable than winters. The map shows us that Santa Barbara is a few degrees farther north than we are here, and San Francisco some few degrees north of that. It is not a tropical but a semi-tropical climate, and for every month in the year you need the same sort of clothing that you wear in New York or Chicago in the winter. He tells me that two-thirds of the year the weather is superb—the heat rarely above sixty-eight degrees and almost always tempered by a refreshing breeze from the ocean or the mountains. Sometimes there are fogs, but they don't bring with them the raw, searching dampness of our eastern ones. Indeed, from all I have heard and read of the climate, I think it would be most beneficial for these patients of mine," Harold concluded, glancing smilingly from one to another.

"And a most enjoyable trip for us all, I have no doubt," said Captain Raymond.

"How about the expenses?" queried Chester.

"Never mind about that," said the captain. "I claim the privilege of bearing it for the party. How many will go?"

"The *Dolphin* could hardly be made to hold us all, papa," laughed Gracie.

"No, nor to cross the plains and mountains," returned her father with an amused smile. "We would go by rail and let those who prefer going home at once do so in our yacht."

At that, Edward Travilla, looking looked greatly pleased, said, "That is a most kind and generous offer, captain, and I for one shall be very glad to accept it. The return trip home will be most pleasant on the *Dolphin*."

"We will consider that you have done so," returned the captain, "and you can begin engaging your passengers as soon as you like. But I am forgetting that I should first learn how many will accept my invitation for the land trip. Grandpa and Grandma Dinsmore, you will do so. Will you not? And you, mother, Cousins Ronald and Annis, too?"

There was a slight demur, a little asking and answering of questions back and forth, which presently ended in a pleased acceptance of the captain's generous invitation by all who had come with him in the *Dolphin* — Violet, his wife, with their children, Elsie and Ned; his older daughters, Lucilla and Gracie with Chester, Lucilla's husband, and Gracie's beloved, Dr. Harold Travilla; Evelyn, Max's wife; and last but not least in importance, Grandma Elsie, Mr. and Mrs. Dinsmore — her father and his wife — and the cousins — Mr. Ronald Lilburn and Annis, his wife.

All had become greatly interested in the trip to the West, and the talk became very cheery and animated. Different possible routes to California were discussed, and it was presently decided to go by the Southern Pacific, taking the cars at

New Orleans. They would make an early start, as would those who were to return home in the *Dolphin*.

"May I take my Tiny along, papa?" asked Elsie, standing by his side with the little monkey upon her shoulder.

"I think not, daughter," he replied. "He would be apt to get lost while we are wandering about in that strange part of the country."

"Then I suppose I'll have to leave him here till we come back. Do you think the servants here would take good care of him and not let him get lost in the woods, papa?" asked the little girl in tones quivering with emotion.

"If you will trust me to take care of him, he can go home with us in the yacht and live at Ion till you come for him," said Zoe. Then, turning to Ned, who was there with his pet, "And I make you the same offer for your Tee-tee," she added. "Of course, if Elsie's can't be trusted to go to California, neither can yours."

"Thank you, Aunt Zoe," both children answered but in tones that told of regret that even for a time they must resign the care of their pets to another.

"And we'll have Tiny and Tee-tee in the yacht with us. How nice that will be!" exclaimed little Eric Leland. "They are fine, amusing little fellows, and you may be sure, Elsie and Ned, that we will take good care of them."

"And be willing to give them back to us when we get home?" asked Elsie.

"Honest enough to do so, I hope, whether we're willing or not," laughed Eric.

"Yes, of course, we would," said his sister, Alie. "We are honest folks, but I'm glad we can have the cute little monkeys with us even for a while."

"On the yacht you will, but I think we'll have them at Ion after we get home," said Lily Travilla, the little daughter of Edward and Zoe. "Because it's papa and mamma who have promised to take care of them."

"Yes," said Elsie, "and I'm sure Uncle Edward and Aunt Zoe will be good to them—so good that I'm most afraid they'll grow fonder of them than of Ned and me."

"Oh, no, I don't think there is any danger of that," said Zoe. "And if they should, you can soon win their hearts back again by your love and kindness."

"Oh, I do believe we can, Aunt Zoe. The dear little things love us now, I'm sure," cried Elsie, giving Tiny a hug and a loving pat.

The older people were chatting about all of the necessary preparations for the journey, and the children grew quiet to listen. Their plans were laid in a few moments, and within twenty-four hours all embarked for New Orleans in the same boat. On reaching that city, the two companies parted, Edward and his charges starting eastward in the *Dolphin*, Captain Raymond and his taking a westward-bound train on the Southern Pacific line.

The little company, especially the younger ones, were in fine spirits. They were pleasant companions for each other, the weather was fine, and the prospect of sightseeing for them seemed quite delightful. The children had many questions to ask about what they should see in California, which the older people, especially their father, were kindly ready to answer.

"What place will we stop first, papa?" asked Elsie.

"At Coronado beach, which is not very far from Los Angeles. We will take rooms at the Hotel del

Coronado, which is an immense building, yet very homelike and delightful. It has an inner court with trees, flowers, and vines, and around that court are many suites of rooms each with its own bath and sitting room. A party of guests such as ours can be very comfortable and as private as they please."

"And if they don't want to be very private, I suppose they can mingle with other folks. Can't they, papa?" asked Ned.

"Yes, indeed. There is almost every kind of amusement that is found elsewhere. Probably fishing and yachting, walking and driving along the beach will suit us as well or better than anything else. There is a drive of twelve miles along the beach at low tide."

"But I fear we will find it too warm for outdoor sports at this time of year," remarked Mrs. Dinsmore pleasantly.

"No, grandma, I think not," said Dr. Harold. "I have been told the summer climate is better than the winter—never too warm for comfort—dry and tempered as it is by the ocean breeze. You do not find there the raw, searching dampness felt at eastern seaside resorts, but I'm told it is too cold for the comfort of invalids during the March rains. They are happily over now, and I think that even our invalids will find the weather comfortably warm."

"And comfortably cool?" queried his mother, giving him a proudly affectionate look and smile.

"I honestly think the ocean breeze will make it that, mother," he answered, returning her smile with one as full of affection as her own.

"I do believe we are going to have a very delightful time," exclaimed Lucilla in joyous tones. "Everything will be so new and fresh—

lovely scenery, beautiful plants and flowers—and the climate all that one could desire."

"Well, I hope you will not be disappointed, my daughter," the captain said. "California is still not heaven, and you must expect some unpleasantness."

"I hope there won't be sicknesses," said Gracie.

"No," said Evelyn sportively, "we must all try to keep well that our good doctor may not be robbed of his vacation."

"My thanks, Mrs. Raymond," said Harold with a bow and smile, "I sincerely hope you will all keep well for your own sakes more than mine."

"You may be sure we will all do our best in that line, Harold, and even more for our own sakes than for yours," laughed Violet.

"I hope so," he returned. "Having persuaded you all to take the trip, I am extremely desirous that it may prove beneficial."

They had been talking during a pause in the movement of the train, and now, as it started on again, they relapsed into silence.

CHAPTER SECOND

THEY ARRIVED AT Coronado Beach tired from their journey but full of delight with the beauty of their surroundings. On the morning after their arrival, they were gathered upon one of the galleries, taking a very interested view of the strange and beautiful scenery spread out before them. The near prospect was of lovely grounds forming the inner court of the hotel—grass trees and hedges of lovely green, borders and oval and beds of marguerites, long lines and curves of marigold, and a fountain encircled by calla lilies. It was beautiful. And farther away they could see other lovely gardens, rocky wastes, lofty mountains, the ocean with distant sails upon it, the beach with foaming waves breaking on it, and Point Loma, grandly guarding the harbor on the right.

"There must be a grand view from the top of that promontory," remarked Chester.

"Yes," said the captain. "Perhaps a call there would be as good a beginning of our peregrinations as we could make. Point Loma commands one of the most remarkable views in the world—an immense prospect and very interesting in its details. I suppose you would all like to go?" he added inquiringly and with a kindly glance from one to another.

No one seemed at all inclined to reject the offered treat, carriages were ordered, and in a few minutes they were on their way.

There was no disappointment. The view from the top of the rocky promontory, Point Loma, was all they had been led to expect—a view of miles of ocean, blue and sparkling in the sunshine and bearing distant vessels on its bosom—and on the land, ranges upon ranges of mountains and away in the distance to the South another promontory, the Point of Rocks in Mexico. They drove along the narrow ridge of the promontory to the lighthouse and found the view very fine from there.

"How beautiful is that wide, curving coast line!" remarked Grandma Elsie.

"Yes, mamma," assented Violet, "and the ranges on ranges of hills and mountains. And there, see, are the snow peaks beyond them. What mountains are they, my dear?"

"San Bernardino and San Jacinto," replied the captain. "That flat-topped one is Table Mountain, which is in Mexico."

"'Tis a grand view, this!" remarked Mr. Lilburn in tones of delight.

"Yes, one of the finest in the world," responded the captain. "What a perfect crescent is that ocean beach, and how singular is the formation of North and South Coronado Beach! Notice the entrance to this harbor here along Point Loma where we are standing and on the spacious inner bay. There are the towns of San Diego and National City. Notice the lowlands and heights outside sprinkled with houses, gardens, vineyards, and orchards."

"It is a beautiful scene," said Mrs. Dinsmore. "The view alone is enough to repay us for our journey."

"Yes, grandma," responded Violet, "especially as the journey itself was really delightful."

"So it was," responded several voices.

"Yes, I think it paid even for giving up my Tiny for a few weeks," said little Elsie. "Are we going anywhere else today, papa?" she asked, turning to her father.

"That is a question I have not considered yet," he answered. "But I think that by the time we get back to the hotel and eat our dinner, it will be rather late for another trip."

"I think so, especially for those of our party who are my patients," said Dr. Travilla. "For a time, I must ask them to avoid both the evening and the early morning air."

"And such is their confidence in your medical wisdom and skill that they will be very apt to take your advice," remarked Lucilla with playful look and tone.

"Certainly we will," added Chester. "What would be the use of bringing a doctor along if his advice is not to be followed?"

"I'm hungry," put in little Ned. "Uncle Harold, wouldn't it be good for us to have something to eat?"

"Why yes, Ned, I highly approve of that fine suggestion," laughed the doctor. "There are lunch baskets in our carriages that will no doubt yield all that is needed to satisfy our appetites."

"Yes, I saw them, Uncle Harold, and so I knew we didn't need to go hungry," replied Ned. Then, turning to his father, "May I go and get the baskets, papa?" he asked. "I s'pose we'll have to eat out here in the open air."

"No doubt we can all eat comfortably enough sitting here on the rocks," replied his father. "But the baskets are too heavy for a boy of your size to carry. We will get one of our drivers to do that." Then addressing the party, "Judging by my own feelings, ladies and gentlemen, I suppose you are all ready for lunch?"

There was a general assent, and presently they were regaling themselves with a very appetizing meal. That concluded, they re-entered their carriages and had a delightful drive back to the Hotel del Coronado, where they passed a pleasant evening and retired early for a comfortable night's rest.

The next day was the Sabbath. The entire party attended morning services at the nearest church, and in the afternoon they spent an hour or more in Bible study together. After that, little Elsie with her Bible in hand drew near Mrs. Travilla.

"Grandma," she said, "I want to ask you about this verse in Revelation. Shall I read it to you?"

"Yes, dear. Let me hear the verse," replied Grandma Elsie softly.

The child read in low, sweet tones, "'He that hath an ear, let him hear what the Spirit saith unto the churches: To him that overcometh will I give to eat of the hidden manna, and will give him a white stone, and in the stone a new name written, which no man knoweth saving he that receiveth it.'"

The little girl paused, closed her Bible, and putting her hand in her pocket, drew out a small white stone.

"See, grandma," she said, "I picked this little stone up yesterday when we were out, and it reminded me of that verse. Please, grandma, tell me what the verse means."

"I will do the best I can, my darling," came the sweet-toned reply. "The white stone was the symbol of acquittal. When a man had been accused or suspected of some crime, tried for it, and found innocent, the judge would give him a white stone, and he could show that as proof that he had been pronounced innocent. The white stone was also the symbol of victory and honor, and it was often given to brave soldiers coming home from battles for their country."

"Then they would be very proud to show it, I suppose," said Elsie. "But was that all the use they had for such stones, grandma?"

"No. They were used as a symbol of friendship. A single stone would be cut in two. One man would take one half, his friend the other, and each would write his name on the piece he held. Then they would exchange them, each keeping his piece with his friend's name upon it as proof and pledge of that friend's love. They might be so separated afterward as not to see or hear from each other for years, and perhaps, if they met again, they would not be able to recognize each other because of changed appearances. The stone would help them to prove their identity and give them the joy of renewed friendship. When they died, their sons would inherit those valuable stones, which would serve as helpers in continuing the friendship of their fathers."

Elsie sat for a moment in thoughtful silence. Then turning to her grandma, she said with a sweet smile, "That was a nice lesson," she said. "Thank you very much for it, grandma."

"What was that, daughter?" asked the captain, approaching them at that moment. In reply, Elsie showed her stone and repeated what her grandma had been telling her.

"That was a very good lesson," said her father. "Keep the little white stone, daughter, and when you look at it remember the Master's promise given with it. Look to Him for strength to overcome, and you will not fail. He says to each one of His children: 'Fear thou not; for I am with thee; be not dismayed, for I am thy God; I will strengthen thee; yea, I will help thee; yea, I will uphold thee with the right hand of my righteousness.' Again and again in that same chapter He repeats His gracious admonition to His people not to fear, because they are His. He is their God and will help them."

"Oh, it is lovely, papa, lovely to belong to Him and know that He will bring us safely all the way through this world to the home with Him that He has prepared for us above!" exclaimed the little girl in joyous tones, her eyes shining with happiness.

At the moment, Violet came in from the gallery, whither all the rest of the party had already gone.

"Come, mamma dear," she said, "we want your company, and we have a comfortable chair placed ready for you. There is plenty of room and a warm welcome, Levis, for you and our little daughter, also," she added, turning her sweet, smiling face toward her husband.

All three promptly accepted her invitation and found it very delightful to gaze upon the beautiful grounds just below them and the sparkling, restless ocean beyond and to inhale the delightful sea breeze — all in the pleasant company of those whose conversation was both interesting and instructive.

The summons to the tea table presently called them away from that pleasant spot, but they returned to it until the approach of bedtime. Then with cordial and kindly goodnights, they separated.

But Lucilla came back presently to find her father pacing the gallery to and fro as was his wont at home. Pausing in his walk, he welcomed her with a smile, put an arm about her, and gave her a kiss that seemed to say she was very dear to him.

"Father," she said, "you were so kind to bring us here to this lovely place."

"Kind to myself as well as to others," he said with a smile. "I am very glad, daughter, to know that you are enjoying it."

"I am, father dear, more that I can find words to express, as is Chester, also. I think the change of climate is improving his health."

"Yes, I think so, and I hope he will go home entirely recovered. Ah, who is this?" as another girlish figure came gliding toward them.

"Another of your daughters, father," answered a sweet-toned voice. "I didn't know you had a companion—though I might have guessed it—and I wanted a bit of chat about your absent son. Isn't it time for letters?"

"Hardly, Eva, my dear, though possibly we may hear tomorrow or next day," replied the captain, putting an arm about her and drawing her close to his side.

"I wish Max could get a furlough and join us here," said Lucilla. "I feel almost mean, Eva, to be enjoying the society of my husband while yours is so far away."

"Oh, Lu, dear, don't feel so," returned Evelyn. "Your happiness certainly does not make mine any less. No, it makes it more. Because, loving you, I rejoice in your happiness."

They chatted together a few moments longer. Then, bidding the captain goodnight, the two young women hastened away to their own rooms.

CHAPTER THIRD

Dr. Travilla, coming out the next morning upon that part of the gallery where their party had spent the previous evening, found Mr. Lilburn and the captain pacing to and fro, chatting and laughing as if enjoying their promenade.

"You see we are far ahead of you, Harold," said the captain when pleasant morning greetings had been exchanged.

"Yes. Very much?" asked Harold.

"Enough for a small stroll around this great building to note its size and architectural features. 'Tis of immense size and well arranged for comfort and convenience."

"And in a delightful situation," supplemented Mr. Lilburn.

"I agree with you both and am entirely willing to spend some days or weeks in it if you wish," returned Harold, "provided the situation agrees with my patients, as I hope and expect it will," he added quickly.

Just then, Lucilla, Evelyn, and Gracie added themselves to the little group, and morning greetings were exchanged. The captain bestowed a fatherly caress upon each daughter—Evelyn being as affectionately greeted as either of the other two.

A few moments later, they were joined by the rest of the party, and all descended together to the dining room to partake of an excellent breakfast. Soon after leaving the table, they went out for the day's sightseeing and adventures. They visited parks, gardens, a museum, an ostrich farm, and a number of other attractive places. Then they took a fine drive along the beach, returning in time for the evening meal at their pleasant house of entertainment.

So delightful did they find Hotel del Coronado that they lingered there for a week.

Then they left it for San Diego, which they found wonderfully beautiful with one of the finest harbors in the world. It was delightful to sit and gaze upon the blue, sunlit bay and breathe in the delicious sea breeze.

Then there were most enjoyable drives to be taken, visiting various attractive spots within a few miles' distance.

One day they drove to Lakeside, twenty-two miles away, where they ate a good dinner at the hotel and wandered across the mesa in its rear, where they had a lovely view of its little lake.

Another day, they drove into the Mont—a large park of a thousand acres. There were great trees—elders, willows, sycamores, and live oaks with enormous trunks and plenty of flowers underneath them and upon the rocks. There were wild peonies with variegated leaves, wild galiardia, tiny starry white flowers, pretty forget-me-nots, and many others too numerous to mention as well as many kinds of beautiful ferns also.

There seemed to be a different drive for every day in the week—all beautiful and enjoyable. So a week passed most pleasantly, and they took the Surf line from San Diego to Los Angeles. It was a seventy-mile ride, but with so much that was interesting to see and gaze upon and such delicious air to breathe, it did not seem a long or wearisome trip. There was the great ocean with its curling, sparkling waves, and seals and porpoises frolicking in the water, gulls circling above them, and from the ground, flocks of birds starting up in affright at the approach of the train. Then when the train carried them away from the view of the ocean, there were the wonderful groves of great trees, carpets of wild flowers, and the towns of Santa Ana and Anaheim.

"What is the name of the place we are going to, papa?" asked Ned, as they drew near the end of their short journey.

"Nuestra Senora la Reina de los Angeles," replied the captain, gravely enough but with a gleam of fun in his eyes.

"What a long name!" cried Ned. "I should think they would have to make it shorter sometimes when they're in a hurry."

"Yes, sometimes it is called 'The City of the Angels,' but even that is too long. So, it commonly goes by the name of Los Angeles."

"Oh, that's better," said Ned, "just a long enough name, I think."

They found Los Angeles a very handsome city environed by gardens filled with beautiful flowers. They spent a few days there and then went on to Pasadena, which was nine miles from Los Angeles, hearing that it was eight hundred feet higher and that the air was much drier. That piece of information drew from Dr. Harold the opinion that the drier air would be even more beneficial for his invalids.

They found a very Eden-like place situated in the beautiful San Gabriel Valley at the foot of the Sierra Madre range of mountains.

"Ah, Pasadena, 'the Crown of the Valley,'" murmured Grandma Elsie delightedly from the carriage window, as they drove to their hotel.

"It looks a veritable paradise," said Violet, "and it reminds me of a description of Pasadena I heard given by a lady at the Hotel del Coronado. She said one would find plenty of flowers in bloom, but at the same time you would need to wear flannels and sealskin sacks. There would be snow-capped mountains and orange blossoms. The trees are green all the year, and you need to go outdoors in December to get warm, where rats build in the trees and squirrels live in the ground with owls."

"And where the boys climb up hills on burros and slide down hills on wheels," laughed Gracie. "I hope we shall see some of those funny things and doings while we are here."

"I hope we shall," said Lucilla. "I particularly want to see the hedges of calla lilies, geraniums, and heliotrope."

"Well, I think we are likely to stay long enough for you all to see whatever there is to be seen," said the captain.

"Yes, I am glad we don't have to hurry away," remarked Gracie in a blithe and cheery tone.

"As we all are, I think," said Grandma Elsie. "I don't know who could fail to desire to stay awhile in so lovely a place as this."

"And we will have nothing to call us away until we are all ready to go," said Captain Raymond.

But their arrival at their house of entertainment brought the conversation to a close.

They found Pasadena so charming that they lingered there week after week. The town was beautiful—protected on three sides by mountain ranges and surrounded by groves and gardens, trees and hedges. There were roses climbing to the tops of houses and covered by tens of thousands of blossoms, and there were passion vines completely covering the arbors. There were hedges made of honeysuckle, the pomegranate, and the heliotrope. Marengo Avenue they found lined on both sides by beautiful pepper trees.

There was a fine hotel called The Raymond, but it was closed at the time. So, these friends, though attracted by the name, could see only the grounds and the outside of the buildings. Set upon a hill commanding a fine view, in the winter season it is filled to overflowing, but it is always closed in April. They found the hill on which it stands an excellent point of view of the country, and itself a mountain of bloom, color and fragrance. It was evident that the views from the windows and broad verandas—views of orchards, gardens, pretty villas, purple foothills, and snowy ranges must be very fine indeed.

"What a beautiful place it is," exclaimed little Elsie when they had gone about the house, viewing it and the grounds from side to side. "I wish it was open so we could stay here. Papa, it has our name. Are the folks who own it related to us?"

"I don't know, daughter, but I hardly think so. It is not an uncommon name," replied the captain.

"It's a good name. I don't want any better," said Ned sturdily.

"I'm glad you are satisfied, and I hope you will never do anything to disgrace it," said his father with a gratified smile and an affectionate pat of the small hand which happened to be held in his at the moment.

The party found a great deal to interest them in and about Pasadena. There were the fine hotels, the pleasant boarding houses, the Public Library in the town, and three miles away the old mission of San Gabriel. They made various trips in the vicinity of the town to Mt. San Jacinto, whose height is twelve thousand feet above the Pacific.

These friends found Pasadena so delightful that they lingered there for some weeks. Then they passed on in a southerly direction till they reached the lovely city of Santa Barbara, where they lingered still longer. They found the place itself wonderfully attractive and the many drives in the vicinity delightful. They found that there were as many as twenty-eight distinct and beautiful drives, and almost every day they tried one or more of them. They greatly enjoyed the scenery — the mountains, the valleys, the beautiful villas with their trees, shrubs, vines and flowers. They saw one grapevine in especial with a trunk eight inches in diameter with foliage covering ten thousand square feet. They were told it yielded in one year twelve thousand pounds of grapes.

Another drive took them to the lighthouse, where from the balcony there was a fine view of the fields below, the blue sea beyond them, and the blue sky overhead. There was hardly anything that the ladies of the party and little Elsie enjoyed more than the sight of the vast profusion of roses — hundreds of varieties and vines covering many feet of arbor and veranda.

Santa Barbara proved a place hard to leave, and they lingered there for a number of weeks. All of them — especially those who had been on the invalid list — feeling that they were constantly gaining in health and strength. News from their homes was favorable to their stay, and everything seemed to be going on very well without them. So they yielded to the fascination of this western fairyland and lingered weeks longer than they had intended when they came.

The summer was nearly over. They began to think it time to be on the move toward home and after a little talk on the subject decided to start the next day, go on to San Francisco, tarry there a few days, then travel eastward to their homes.

Evelyn was the most eager for the start. It seemed so long since she had last seen her young husband, and they were hoping he might get a furlough and spend some weeks with her at Crag Cottage, their pretty home on the Hudson.

They tarried in San Francisco long enough to acquaint themselves with all its beauties then wended their way eastward as fast as the cars could carry them. They felt it still too early in the season for an immediate return to their southern homes, but they scattered to various places in the north — some to visit relatives, some to the seaside, while several accepted an invitation from Evelyn to spend some weeks at Crag Cottage. She knew that her aunt, Elsie Leland, was already there, and they had everything in order for their reception. Grandma Elsie, Dr. Harold Travilla, Gracie Raymond, and her sister, Lucilla, were the others who accepted the invitation. But Captain Raymond, Violet, and their younger children expected to visit for some weeks one of Long Island's seaside resorts.

Max had written to Evelyn that he hoped for a furlough that would enable him to join her at the cottage and spend with her the few weeks she would care to stay there. She was looking forward to that reunion with eager delight while journeying from California to the home of her childhood.

"Father and Mamma Vi," she said to them as they journeyed through the state of New York, "stop with me at Crag Cottage and make at least a little visit there. I think you will see Max if you do. I have a good feeling that he will be there to meet us upon our arrival."

"Thank you, daughter," returned Captain Raymond with a look of pleasure, "I shall be happy to accept your invitation, if it suits my wife to do so. What do you say, Violet, my dear?"

"That I accept gladly! I shall be pleased to see both Max and the pretty cottage and to be Eva's guest for a few days."

"What will Elsie and I do?" asked Ned with a roguish look. "Go on to the seashore by ourselves?"

"No, little brother, we wouldn't any of us be willing to trust you to do that," laughed Evelyn. "And as large as you are, I think the cottage can be made to hold you two in addition to the others."

"Oh, good! I'm glad of that, for I always enjoy a visit to Crag Cottage," cried Ned, clapping his hands in glee.

"And I hope you will be often there visiting your brother and sister," said Evelyn, smiling affectionately and patting the hand he had laid upon the arm of her seat.

Her invitation was not extended to the other members of the party, as their plans were already made. Mr. and Mrs. Lilburn had already left them to visit their relatives at Pleasant Plains, and Mr. and Mrs. Horace Dinsmore had announced their intentions of visiting their relatives in the neighborhood of Philadelphia.

"We will reach New York presently," remarked the captain after a little. "There we will leave the train and go aboard the *Dolphin*, if, as I have every reason to expect, she is lying at the dock there. We can all journey up to Crag Cottage in her."

"Which will be a pleasant change from travelling on land in a car," remarked Lucilla.

"You will go with us. Will you not, Chester?" asked Evelyn.

"Thank you," he returned heartily. "I must leave my wife with you and hurry home to attend to some professional matters that I have neglected too long in my desire to fully recover my health."

"Be careful that you don't lose it again," said Dr. Travilla, warningly.

"Yes, for your wife's sake be careful," urged Lucilla, a look of anxiety on her usually happy face.

"You must trust me for that, I think," Chester returned laughingly. A few hours later, they reached New York, and as they left the train, Evelyn was overjoyed to find herself in her husband's arms. His furlough had been granted. He had already been aboard the *Dolphin* and was able to assure them that everything there and at Crag Cottage was in order for their reception.

They had already bade good-bye to Mr. and Mrs. Horace Dinsmore, who were going on at once to Philadelphia, and Chester went with them as far as that city. So the party for the *Dolphin* went aboard of her without any unnecessary delay and immediately journeyed in her up to their desired haven.

It was a short voyage made doubly pleasant by the happy reunion of near and dear ones. It was a great joy to Max to have his wife again by his side and father, stepmother, sisters, and brother close at hand. All showed obvious delight in the reunion and great affection for him. The presence of Grandma Elsie and her son, the good and lovable physician, was by no means a drawback upon the felicity of any one of them.

A most joyous and affectionate greeting awaited them all on reaching their destination. Mr. and Mrs. Leland and their sons and daughters were evidently delighted at their arrival—a natural consequence of the many ties of kinship existing among them.

Mrs. Leland had done her part well. She had capable servants under her. The house was in beautiful order, and the table well served. Several days passed most delightfully—mostly on shore, though some little trips were taken in the yacht. Then the Raymonds began to talk of leaving, but they were urged to stay on a little longer.

CHAPTER FOURTH

IT WAS EARLY morning, the sun just peeping over the mountaintops on the farther side of the river when Captain Raymond might have been seen pacing to and fro in the beautiful grounds of Crag Cottage. Now and then he glanced toward the open hall door, expecting that Lucilla would join him in his early stroll as she so often did. Presently some one did step out and hasten toward him. It was not Lucilla, however, but Dr. Harold Travilla.

"Good morning, Grandpa Raymond," was Harold's greeting with a bow and a smile.

"What?" cried the captain in a loud voice, standing still in surprise.

"A pretty little girl has just arrived, scarcely an hour ago, and as Max claims to be her father, I take it that Max's father must be her grandsire."

"Ah! An astonishing bit of news! She was not expected so soon?"

"No, not for some weeks yet, but the parents are very happy over her prompt arrival. So far both mother and child are doing well."

"That is good news. All you have told me is good news, although it seems a little odd to think of myself as a grandfather," remarked the captain with a smile. Then turning to Lucilla, who joined them at that moment, he told the news to her.

"Oh," she cried, "how nice! Harold, can I go in now, speak to Eva, and look at her treasure?"

"Not yet," he said. "She needs rest, and I think she is sleeping. We will let you in some hours later."

"Thank you. I certainly don't want to go to her until her physician considers it quite safe to do so," returned Lucilla.

"Nor do I," said the captain, "though I shall be pleased to get sight of my first grandchild."

"Oh, yes, she has made you a grandfather, papa," laughed Lucilla. "How odd that seems!"

"You, Gracie, and Elsie—aunts and Ned—my little Ned—an uncle."

"Oh, won't he be tickled!" laughed Lucilla.

"We will see," laughed the captain, "for here he comes," as Ned was seen at that very moment approaching them in their walk.

"Good morning, papa and Sister Lu," he cried, as he drew near. "Good morning, Uncle Harold."

"Good morning," returned his father. "Have you heard the news?"

"News, papa? No, sir. What is it?" he asked, putting his hand into that of his father. "Nothing bad, I guess, 'cause you looked pleased and so do sister and uncle."

"I hope you, too, will be pleased when you hear it," said his father. "You have a little niece, Ned. You are an uncle."

"Oh, am I? Why, how did it happen? Where is she now?"

"She is only a little baby," laughed Lucilla. "Brother Max and Sister Eva are her father and mother, Ned."

"And God gave her to them an hour ago," added their father. "I want you to remember to make no noise anywhere about the house, because your Sister Eva is not well and noise would be very apt to make her worse."

"Yes, sir, I think I can remember to be quiet so as not to hurt Sister Eva or wake the baby if she is asleep. I'd like to see her, though."

"I think we will all be treated to a sight of her before very long," said the captain.

"Oh," cried Ned, "there are mamma and Elsie on the porch. Let's go and tell them the good news."

And away he ran followed by his father and Sister Lu.

"Oh, mamma, have you heard the news?" he cried, as he came panting up the steps.

"That I am a grandmother and you an uncle?" she asked with a merry laugh.

"Why, no, mamma! You are not old enough to be that," exclaimed Elsie.

"No, indeed!" cried Ned. "But papa is now a grandfather, and Lu and Gracie and Elsie are aunts, and I'm an uncle. Oh, isn't it funny?"

"I hope you will be a well-behaved uncle and not make your little niece ashamed of you," laughed Violet pleasantly.

"I guess she won't be," returned Ned. "Anyhow, not till she gets bigger. She's just a little baby now, papa says."

Captain Raymond and Lucilla were now coming up the porch steps, and at the same moment Max stepped out onto the porch from the hall door. He was looking very happy.

"Good morning, father," he said. "And a good morning to you, too, Mamma Vi, and all of you. Father, I suppose Harold has told you all the wonderful news?"

"Yes, my dear boy. It is very pleasant news, though it seems to add something to my age to know myself a grandfather," returned the captain with a smile, taking Max's extended hand in a warm pressure.

"What did you choose a girl for, Brother Max?" asked Ned. "I should think you'd rather have a boy. Wouldn't you?"

"No, little brother," laughed Max. "I'm glad it is a girl, and I always shall be glad, if she grows up to be just like her mother, as I hope she will."

"I hope so, too, Max, and I am well pleased that she is a girl," said Lucilla. "But I am glad that father and mother had a boy first so that I have always had an older brother to look up to."

"And you have really looked up to him?" laughed Max. "I haven't always known it, and I certainly have not always been worthy of it."

Just then, they were joined by Grandma Elsie and her daughter, Mrs. Leland with her husband and children.

All had heard the good news and were full of the subject. The ladies and children wanted to see the little newcomer, but that could not be for the present without running the risk of disturbing her mother. Just then came the summons to the breakfast table.

Dr. Harold was with them there, and on being questioned, he spoke in a cheerful, hopeful way of his patient.

"I left her asleep," he said, "and looking very peaceful and comfortable with the bit lassie reposing by her side. The nurse seems a very capable one, and I think she will take the best care of both mother and babe."

"When can we see Eva and the baby, Uncle Harold?" asked little Elsie.

"After her mother wakes, yours and mine will probably carry her out into the dressing room for a few minutes. Then, if you two will engage to be very quiet, you may go in there and take a peep at the little nameless stranger," replied the doctor.

"Nameless!" exclaimed Elsie. "Oh, Brother Max, what are you going to name her?"

"Her mother shall name her. I am sure she has the best right," replied Max.

"So I think," said his father. "Violet, my dear, how soon will you and the children be ready for our trip down the river?"

"I think I can make ready in an hour or two at any time," Violet answered with a smile.

"Oh, father, please don't think of leaving us!" exclaimed Max. "I am absolutely hungry for a good visit with you, and you have had sea air for months past. Besides, there is plenty of room here and of everything else that is wanted. I hope you will stay until Eva and I are ready to go."

"Thank you, my son," the captain said, giving Max a look of fatherly pride and pleasure. "A few weeks of your society will be far from disagreeable to your old father. So, Violet," turning to her, "shall we accept his invitation?"

"Yes, with the understanding that if at any time we prove troublesome company, we are to be informed that such is the case and to leave at very short notice."

"You may be sure of getting such notice if your conduct calls for it," laughed Mrs. Leland. "So don't set your heart too strongly upon staying here as long as Max and Eva do."

"There is not the slightest danger of Sister Violet earning such notice and hardly of her children doing so," remarked Mr. Leland, "but I am not so sure of our own boys and girls. Remember, my children," glancing around upon them, "that you are to play very quietly when you are in or near the house while Cousin Eva is sick."

In answer, there was a chorus of assurances that they would be very careful to do nothing to injure "dear Cousin Eva," but everything they could to help her to get well.

An hour later they were all—including Elsie and Ned—invited to go quietly into Cousin Eva's dressing room and see her new treasure, whom they found sleeping on Grandma Elsie's lap. They all regarded her with great interest and pronounced her a dear, pretty little thing.

"What is her name, grandma?" they asked.

"I don't think she has any yet, except that she is a little Miss Raymond," Grandma Elsie answered with a smile and a loving look down at the wee face.

"Oh, yes, because Brother Max is her father and his name is Raymond," said little Elsie. "Sisters Lu and Gracie and I are her aunts. Oh, I think it's nice to have such a dear little niece!"

"Or cousin," said Eric Leland. "I can't be her uncle, but she's my cousin, because her mother is."

"Yes," said Grandma Elsie. "So she is, and I hope you will be so kind to her that she cannot help loving you. Now you may all go out into the grounds and enjoy yourselves there far enough from the house not to disturb your sick cousin if you want to make any noise."

"I think we will all try to be quiet, grandma," said Elsie, "and go far enough away not to disturb Sister

Eva with our talk." And with that, they all moved out of the room very quietly.

Elsie led the way to the summerhouse on the edge of the cliff, which had always been one of Evelyn's favorite resorts. There they seated themselves, enjoying the beautiful prospect of the river and its farther shore.

"That baby is a dear, pretty little cousin for us all. Isn't she?" remarked Alie Leland.

"To you and your sister and brothers," Elsie answered with a merry look and tone. "But she is niece to Ned and me, you must remember, because her father is our brother."

"Well, I don't care," laughed Alie. "I believe it's about as good to be cousin as aunt."

CHAPTER FIFTH

EVA AWOKE FROM a long, quiet sleep to find her husband sitting close by her side and gazing upon her as if he thought her the greatest of earthly treasure.

"Dear Max," she said, smiling up into his eyes, "it is so sweet to have you so close, keeping guard over me as if I were the dearest of earthly possessions."

"That is just what you are, love," he returned, leaning over her and kissing lip and cheek and brow. "And this little darling comes next," he added, looking down at the sleeping babe close by her side.

"Ah, she is a treasure, oh, such a treasure to me, but I am sorry for your sake that she is only a girl."

"Only a girl!" he exclaimed. "I am glad she is that. I would not have her anything else, and I hope she will prove a second edition of her mother."

"Thank you, my dear," Eva said with a smile. "But she must have a name, and what shall it be?"

"Whatever pleases her mother," replied Max, returning the smile.

"No, I think the decision should rest with her father," Eva said with her low, sweet laugh.

"Shall we call her Elsie for your good, kind aunt?" returned Max.

"I should like to give that token of affection to both her and her mother," said Evelyn, "were it not that there are already so many little Elsies in the connection. How would Mary do? Or shorten it to May."

"Quite well, I think," said Max. "So let us call her our little May."

"Little treasure!" murmured Evelyn, gazing upon the baby face. "Oh, Max, I feel it very sweet to be a mother—to have a little darling of my very own."

"And I find it far from unpleasant to be a father," he returned merrily, "the only drawback upon my felicity being the hard fact that I must leave my two dearest ones so often for my life upon the sea."

"Ah," she sighed, "I must try not to think of that now. It is a hard thought, though I am proud of my husband's readiness to serve his country."

"A country well worth serving, I think," smiled Max, "the grandest one in the world."

Doctor and nurse both came in at that moment.

"In which opinion I heartily agree with you," said Harold, having overheard Max's last sentence. "But remember, my good naval officer, that you must not talk in too exciting a way to my patient."

"Oh, I am not at all excited, but if you abuse my husband I shall be," said Evelyn with a mirthful look and tone.

"Oh, I am not abusing him or intending to," said Harold, "but my patient's welfare must always receive my first consideration."

"Pleasant doctrine for me while I am the patient," laughed Evelyn.

Harold was looking at the sleeping babe. "She's a pretty bit lassie for one of her age," he said. "I hope one of these days to claim her as my niece."

"So you may. I think you will suit very well for an uncle," laughed Max, "an uncle for my child since you have ceased to be one for myself."

"Yes, I prefer to be your brother," was Harold's response to that.

"Gracie is much pleased with her little niece," said Evelyn, "and with the thought of being an aunt, as Lucilla is, also."

"Yes, and the little cousins, too," said Grandma Elsie, coming in at that moment. "Ah, she is waking now. See, her eyes are open. Suppose you let me carry her into the dressing room again and let them refresh their eyes with another sight of the dear, little face."

"Agreed, Grandma Elsie, if you will let me go along to witness the scene," said Max. "I'll carry her very carefully on a pillow."

He did so and laid her on Grandma Elsie's lap, she having seated herself in a low, easy chair. Then the children were notified and gathered about her in an eager, excited group, while the young father stood near looking on.

"I wish I might hold her in my arms for a little," said Alie Leland.

"No, I'm too young. Don't touch me, cousins," the baby seemed to say.

"Oh, she can talk! She can talk!" cried Alie Leland.

"The same way that the tee-tees did," laughed her brother, Edward.

"But Cousin Ronald isn't even here," exclaimed several childish voices.

"No, but Cousin Max is, and he is a ventriloquist, too," returned Edward, looking smilingly at the baby's father.

"Well, now, Ned," said Max, "do you really think my little girl is not capable of saying a few words for herself?"

"Oh, I daresay she will talk fast enough some of these days," laughed the lad, "but I know babies don't talk when they are hardly a week old."

"Except when there's a ventriloquist at hand," said Eric.

"Brother Max," exclaimed Ned, "I'm so glad you are a ventriloquist, because I hope you'll make a good deal of fun for us, as Cousin Ronald does."

"Isn't it enough for me to help my little girl talk?" asked Max.

"That's good," said Ned. "Please make her talk some more."

"No, you talk, Uncle Ned," the baby seemed to say. "I'm tired."

Ned laughed and shouted, "There! She called me uncle, grandma! She's a nice baby. Isn't she?"

"I think so," replied Mrs. Travilla, "and we must all be careful to teach her by example only what is good and lovable."

Violet and Lucilla came into the dressing room together at that moment.

"I must have a good look at my little niece," said the latter.

"And I at my granddaughter," added Violet.

"Oh, mamma, don't say that," exclaimed Elsie. "You are far too young for it. Isn't she, grandma?"

"She does look rather young to lay claim to that appellation," Grandma Elsie returned with an admiring smile up into her daughter's beautiful and youthful face.

"Ah, but her own grandsire being my husband gives me something of a right in that direction," laughed Violet. "And anybody might be glad to claim kinship with such a darling," she added, gazing down at the babe as it lay on Grandma Elsie's knee.

"Thank you, Grandma Vi," came in a feeble little voice, apparently from the lips of the babe.

At that moment, the captain entered the room.

"Ah, so my little granddaughter is on exhibition, I see," he said, as he approached the little group gathered about Grandma Elsie and the babe.

"Yes, grandpa," she seemed to say. "My papa helps me to talk."

"Does he? I'm afraid you will lose your ability to talk when he goes away," said the captain, bending down over the babe and gazing with loving admiration into the wee face. "She's a fine child, I think, Max," he said, "one that I am proud to claim as my grandchild."

"She doesn't seem to appreciate your praise, my dear," said Violet, as the child began to squirm and cry.

At that, her nurse came and took charge of her, and her visitors vanished to other parts of the house and grounds.

CHAPTER SIXTH

THE NEXT DAY was the Sabbath, and all who were not needed in the sick room attended church in the morning. In the afternoon, according to their old custom, they assembled together as a Bible class with the captain being the leader. The subject was the New Jerusalem, its beauties, its delights, and the character and bliss of its inhabitants. "They will be very happy there," said the captain. "In Isaiah we read, 'Behold, my servants shall sing for joy of heart . . . Behold, I create new heavens and a new earth: and the former shall not be remembered nor come into mind. But be ye glad, and rejoice in that which I create: for, behold, I create Jerusalem a rejoicing and her people a joy. And I will rejoice in Jerusalem, and joy in my people . . . and the voice of weeping shall be no more heard in her, nor the voice of crying.' Mother, can you give us a text from the New Testament teaching that there is no weeping in heaven?"

"Yes," replied Grandma Elsie, "in the twenty-first chapter and fourth verse of Revelation we read: 'And God shall wipe away all tears from their eyes; and there shall be no more death, neither sorrow, nor crying, neither shall there be any more pain: for the former things are passed away.' It was sin," she said, "that brought sorrow, pain, sickness, and death into the world. There will be none of any of those in the New Jerusalem."

"Will some one give us a Bible description of the New Jerusalem?" asked the captain.

"I will read it, father," said Gracie. "'And He carried me away in the spirit to a great and high mountain, and shewed me that great city, the holy Jerusalem, descending out of heaven from God, having the glory of God: and her light was like unto a stone most precious, even like a jasper stone, clear as crystal; and had a wall great and high, and had twelve gates, and at the gates twelve angels, and names written thereon, which are the names of the twelve tribes of the children of Israel: On the east three gates; on the north three gates; on the south three gates; and on the west three gates. And the wall of the city had twelve foundations, and in them the names of the twelve apostles of the Lamb. And he that talked with me had a golden reed to measure the city, and the gates thereof . . . And the city lieth foursquare, and the length is as large as the breadth: and he measured the city with the reed twelve thousand furlongs. The length and the breadth and the height of it are equal. And he measured the wall thereof, an hundred and forty and four cubits, according to the measure of a man, that is, of the angel. And the building of the wall of it was of jasper: and the city was pure gold, like unto clear glass. And the foundations of the wall of the city were garnished with all manner of precious stones. The first foundation was jasper; the second, sapphire; the third, a chalcedony; the fourth, an emerald; the fifth, sardonyx; the sixth, sardius; the seventh, chrysolyte; the eighth, beryl; the ninth, a topaz; the tenth, a chrysoprasus; the eleventh, a jacinth; the twelfth, an amethyst. And the twelve gates were twelve pearls; every several gate was of one pearl: and the street of the city was pure gold, as it were transparent glass. And I saw no temple therein: for the Lord God Almighty and the Lamb are the temple of it. And the city had no need of the sun, neither of the moon, to shine in it: for the glory of God did lighten it, and the Lamb is the light thereof. And the nations of them which are saved shall walk in the light of it: and the kings of the earth do bring their glory and honour into it. And the gates of it shall not be shut at all by day: for there shall be no night there. And they shall bring the glory and honour of the nations into it. And there shall in no wise enter into it any thing that defileth, neither whatsoever worketh abomination, or maketh a lie: but they which are written in the Lamb's book of life.'"

"What a beautiful, glorious city it will be!" she exclaimed when she had finished.

"Yes," said her father. "God grant we may all be numbered among its citizens."

"'Looking for that blessed hope and the glorious appearing of the great God and our Savior, Jesus Christ,'" quoted Mr. Leland. "We may well look for it with joyful longing. May the goodness and love of God lead us all to repentance and make us all His devoted, faithful servants."

"And He will be the same Jesus who gave His life for us," said Grandma Elsie in a voice tremulous with emotion. "The angels said to those who were gazing up after Him as He was taken up into heaven and a cloud received Him out of their sight, 'Ye men of Galilee, why stand ye gazing up into heaven? This same Jesus which is taken up from you into heaven shall so come in like manner as ye have seen Him go into heaven.'"

"Yes," said Harold, "and we are told in Thessalonians that the Lord Himself shall descend from heaven and in Revelation, 'Behold, He cometh with clouds; and every eye shall see Him.' And Matthew tells us, 'The Son of Man shall come in His glory, and all the holy angels with Him.'"

"And we shall see Him, know Him, and at last be conformed to His image," said Mrs. Travilla in joyous tones. "'It doth not yet appear what we shall be: but we know that, when He shall appear, we shall be like Him; for we shall see Him as He is.'"

"What a delightful thought!" exclaimed her daughter, Mrs. Leland. "Oh, it is strange that we can ever be so taken up as we are with worldly matters. Do you think, captain, that His second coming is near?"

"There are many things that make it seem highly probable," replied Captain Raymond. "Don't you think that we should try to live as if it might be any day — or indeed at any moment?"

"I certainly do," she answered, "especially as death may take any one of us into His presence at any moment."

"Yes, that is true," he answered. "We should all strive to live as when death comes we shall wish we had. Live near to Him — to His honor and glory — that whenever He shall come we may be found ready. He tells us, 'Watch, therefore, for ye know not what hour your Lord doth come . . . Be ye also ready: for in such an hour as ye think not the Son of Man cometh.' That warning word 'watch' is repeated again and again. 'Watch, therefore; for ye know neither the day nor the hour wherein the Son of Man cometh.'"

"'Be ye also ready,'" repeated Elsie Raymond reflectively. "Papa, please tell us just how to get ready—just what we must do."

"Give ourselves to the Lord Jesus who says, 'Him that cometh unto Me I will in no wise cast out.' 'God so loved the world, that He gave His only begotten Son, that whosoever believeth in Him should not perish, but have everlasting life.' 'Believe on the Lord Jesus Christ, and thou shalt be saved.'"

"Doesn't everybody believe that it's all true about Him, papa?" asked Ned.

"It is not enough to believe simply that Jesus lived in this world years ago and died the cruel death of crucifixion. We must believe that He was God as well as man, for otherwise He could not save us. Had He been only a man, His death would not have atoned for the sins of the world—or of all in it who had believed or will believe on Him. But the Bible tells us these things as plainly as words can speak. In the first chapter of John's Gospel, we are told, 'In the beginning was the Word, and the Word was with God, and the Word was God. The same was in the beginning with God. All things were made by Him, and without Him was not anything made that was made.' And Jesus Himself said, 'I and my father are one.'"

"Yes," said Mrs. Leland, "it is incomprehensible to me how any one can profess to believe the Bible to be the Word of God and deny the divinity of Christ—so plainly is that taught in it again and again."

CHAPTER SEVENTH

THE DAYS GLIDED by very pleasantly to the little company at Crag Cottage — the greater part of them passed by the children in the open air far enough from the house to make them feel sure of not disturbing Evelyn, even if they indulged in rather loud chat and laughter.

In the evenings, if the air was not too cool, all usually gathered upon the porch overlooking the river, and they were very apt to be entertained with a fine story from either Grandma Elsie or Captain Raymond.

"I'm right glad to be where I can see this grand old Hudson River," remarked Edward Leland one evening as they sat there. "It is a beautiful stream, and so much happened on it in early days."

"What in particular are you thinking of now?" asked his mother.

"Something I read not so very long ago in Lossing's *Field Book of the Revolution*. He tells of things that happened to Putnam nearly twenty years before that war. He was lying in a bateau on the east side of the river above the rapids when he was suddenly surprised by a group of Indians. He couldn't cross the river quickly enough to escape the danger from their rifles. So the only way to save himself from being killed or taken prisoner — which I suppose would have amounted to the same thing—was to go over those dangerous rapids. It took Putnam but an instant to decide. He steered directly down the current between whirling eddies and over shelving rocks, cleared them all in a few moments, and was gliding along the smooth current below far out of the reach of the Indians' weapons. They would never have dared go over those falls as he did. So they thought he must have been favored by the Great Spirit and that if they should try to kill him with powder and ball, that Great Spirit would consider it an affront to him.

"Putnam was certainly a very, very brave man," continued the lad. "Lossing tells of a brave deed of his at Fort Edward. He says that in the winter of 1756, the barracks took fire, and the magazine, which contained three hundred barrels of gunpowder, was only twelve feet distant from the blaze. Men attempted to knock down the barracks with heavy cannon, but they failed.

"Putnam, who was stationed on Roger's Island in the Hudson opposite the fort, must have seen the fire. He hurried over there, took his station on the roof of the barracks, and ordered a line of soldiers to hand him water. He did his best but could not put the fire out. It drew nearer and nearer to the magazine. Colonel Haviland, seeing his danger, ordered him down, but he was too brave and persevering to obey that order. He worked on and would not leave his post until the building began to totter as if just ready to fall. Then he jumped to the ground and put himself between it—the falling barracks—and the magazine and poured on water with all his might. The outside planks of the magazine were already burned so that there was only a thin partition between the fire and the powder, but he did succeed in extinguishing the flames and saving the powder."

"But wasn't he dreadfully burned?" asked Elsie.

"Yes, his hands and face were," replied Edward, "and his whole body more or less blistered—so much so that it was several weeks before he fully recovered from the bad effects of that fight."

"He must have been a very brave man," cried Ned Raymond.

"He was," said Grandma Elsie. "Would you all like to hear something more about him and his brave doings?"

"Yes, indeed, grandma, if you will be pleased to tell the story," answered several young voices, and at once she began.

"He was a Massachusetts man and had a fine, large farm, where he paid particular attention to the raising of fruits and of sheep. There had been a good many wild beasts in that region, but in 1735, all seemed to have been killed except an old female wolf that for some seasons went on visiting the farmyards and killing the fowls. Her lair was near Putnam's farm, and one night she killed sixty or seventy of his fine sheep. Of course, a company was promptly raised to search for her and kill her. They tracked her to her lair in a cave. It was dark and narrow, but Putnam pursued her into it, shot her at short range, and dragged her out in triumph.

"Twenty years after that in 1755, troops were raised to defend the country against the French, and Putnam was given the rank of captain. He became a leading member of the band of Rangers that did much to annoy and embarrass the enemy during the next two years. In 1757, he was promoted to the rank of major, and after that occurred the two events Edward has just given us.

"In August of 1758, he was taken prisoner by the Indians after a sharp skirmish near Wood Creek. The Indians tortured him, and then decided they would burn him alive. They stripped him, bound him to a tree, and kindled a fire about him. The flames were searing his flesh when Captain Moland, a French officer, came rushing through the crowd, scattered the firebrands, cuffed and upbraided the Indians, and released poor Putnam."

"Did he get away from the Indians?" asked Elsie.

"He was taken to Montreal and soon afterward exchanged," replied her grandma. "Afterward, he was promoted to a lieutenant-colonelcy and given command of a regiment.

"The next year he was with General Amherst in his march from Oswego to Montreal. When going down the St. Lawrence River, they found it desirable to dislodge the French from Fort Oswegatchie, but the approach to it was guarded by two schooners, the larger one having twelve guns, which could have done serious damage to the English boats. Thinking of that danger, General Amherst said, 'I wish there were some way of taking that schooner.' 'All right,' said Putnam. 'Just give me some wedges and a mallet, and a half dozen men of my own choosing, and I'll soon take her for you.'

"The British general smiled incredulously, evidently not believing the thing could be done. But he consented to Putnam's making the proposed attempt, and in the night Putnam and his little party got into a light boat and, with muffled oars, rode under the schooner's stern and drove the wedges between the rudder and the stern-post so firmly as to render the helm unmanageable. They then went around under the bow, cut the vessel's cable, and rowed quietly away. All that, of course, made the vessel unmanageable. She drifted ashore before morning and struck her colors. Then the other French vessels surrendered, and the English captured the fort.

"But I shall not attempt to tell the story of the services of Putnam's whole life," continued Grandma Elsie. "I suppose what you all care particularly to hear is of what he did and suffered in and after the Revolution."

"Yes, grandma. Yes, indeed!" replied several voices, and she continued her story.

"In August of 1774, before General Gage had quite shut up the approaches to Boston, Putnam rode over the Neck with one hundred sheep as a gift from the parish of Brooklyn. While there, he was the guest of Dr. Warren. On the twentieth of the next April came the news of the fight at Concord."

"Ah! News didn't fly so fast then as it does now," remarked Eric.

"No, not by any means," assented his grandma. "Putnam was in the field ploughing when the news reached him. So great was his excitement on hearing it that he left his plough in the furrow, and without waiting to put on his uniform, he mounted a horse and rode toward Cambridge, reaching there at sunrise of the next morning. Later in the same day, he was at Concord. But he was soon summoned to Hartford to consult with the Connecticut legislature. He returned from there with the chief command of the forces of that colony, and the rank of brigadier."

"He was one of the officers at the battle of Bunker Hill. Wasn't he, grandma?" asked Eric.

"Yes, he is spoken of as the ranking officer, and it was he who had the earthworks thrown up on the crest of Bunker Hill in the rear, and who, toward the close of the day, conducted the retreat and directed the fortifying of Prospect Hill."

"And his rank was soon made still higher by Congress. Was it not, grandma?" asked Edward.

"Yes. In June of 1775, Congress appointed Washington to the chief command and made Ward, Lee, Schuyler, and Putnam major-generals. Putnam was in command for a time in New York, in Philadelphia, and in Princeton. Afterward, he had charge of the defense of the highlands of the Hudson River with his headquarters at Peekskill.

"There took place an occurrence that will no doubt interest you all. A man named Edmund Palmer was caught lurking in the American camp and condemned to death as a spy.

"The British considered American spies worthy of death but that those in the king's service were not. So, Sir Henry Clinton sent up a flag of truce from New York and a threat to Putnam of signal vengeance should he dare to injure the person of the king's liege subject, Edmund Palmer.

"The old general's reply was brief and to the point. I think I can recall it word for word: 'Headquarters, 7th of August, 1777. Edmund Palmer, an officer in the enemy's service, was taken as a spy lurking within our lines. He has been tried as a spy, condemned as a spy, and shall be executed as a spy, and the flag is ordered to depart immediately. —Israel Putnam. P.S. He has accordingly been executed.'"

"I daresay Sir Henry Clinton was very angry when he read that note. Wasn't he?" asked Eric.

"Yes," said his brother, "but no doubt it was well for Putnam that Sir Henry never had power to carry out his threat of vengeance upon him."

"Is that all of the story about him, grandma?" asked Ned Raymond.

"Yes," she replied, "except that there is a story of a remarkable escape of his from General Tryon's troops by riding down a flight of stone steps at Horseneck, or West Greenwich, in the town of Greenwich, Connecticut. He was visiting his outposts there, staying at the house of General Mead. It was the twenty-sixth of March, early in the morning, and he was standing before a looking glass shaving when he saw in the glass the reflection of a body of redcoats marching up the road from the westward. Though only half shaven, he dropped his razor, buckled on his sword, and, hurrying out, mounted his horse and hastened to prepare his handful of men to oppose the approaching enemy. There were nearly fifteen hundred of the British regulars and Hessians under General Tryon. Putnam had with him only 150 men. He arranged them upon the brow of the hill near a church in the village. There he planted a battery composed of two old iron field pieces, and he waited for the coming of the enemy.

"They came up in a solid column until almost within musket shot. Then detachments were broken off and tried to gain the American's flanks. At the same time, the British dragoons and some infantry made ready to charge. Perceiving that and noting the overwhelming numbers of the enemy, Putnam ordered a retreat after some volleys of musketry and a few discharges of the field pieces. But the enemy was so near that the retreat of the Americans became a rout. The soldiers broke and fled singly to the adjacent swamps, and the general, putting spurs to his horse, hastened toward Stamford, being pursued by several of the dragoons.

"About a quarter of a mile distant from Putnam's starting on that ride is a steep declivity. On the brow of that, the road turned northward and passed, in a broad sweep, round the hill. Putnam, seeing that his pursuers were gaining on him, took a desperate resolve, left the road, and wheeled his horse, while on a gallop, down the rocky height, making a zigzag course to the bottom and reaching the road again in safety."

"And did the dragoons follow him, grandma?" asked Ned.

"No," she said, "it was too perilous for them. They did not dare attempt it. They fired their pistols at Putnam but did not succeed in wounding him. He rode on in safety to Stamford."

"Was Putnam good to his soldiers, grandma?" asked Elsie.

"I think he was," Mrs. Travilla answered. "He felt for them in their sore privations and tried to get them help. Lossing tells us that in a letter to Washington in January of 1778, he gives a picture of the terrible suffering that his soldiers in the highlands were enduring. He said: 'Very few have either a shoe or a shirt, and most of them have neither stockings, breeches, nor overalls. Several companies of enlisted artificers are in the same situation and unable to work in the field.' Lossing tells us of something similar that occurred at Reading, Connecticut the next year — in 1779. The troops, poor fellows, were badly fed and clothed and worse paid, for their small pittance when it came was in the form of Continental money, which was depreciating rapidly. Brooding over their hard lot and talking the matter over among themselves, they resolved to march to Hartford and demand of the assembly there a redress of their grievances. The second brigade had assembled under arms with that intention when Putnam learned what was going on. He at once galloped to the encampment, and earnestly addressed them: 'My brave lads, where are you going?' he asked. 'Do you intend to desert your officers and to invite the enemy to follow you into the country? Whose cause have you been fighting and suffering so long for? Is it not your own? Have you no property, no parents, wives, or children? You have behaved like men so far; all the world is full of your praise, and prosperity will stand astonished at your deeds, but not if you spoil all at last. Don't you consider how much the country is distressed by the war, and that your officers have not been better paid than yourselves? But we all expect better times and that the country will do us ample justice. Let us all stand by one another, then, and fight it out like brave soldiers. Think what a shame it would be for Connecticut men to run away from their officers.' That was Putnam's little speech, and when he had finished, the discontented regiments cheered him loudly and returned to their quarters in good humor, resolved still to suffer and fight for the cause of their country."

"Poor fellows!" sighed Elsie.

"Did Putnam live till the Revolutionary War was over, grandma?" asked Eric.

"Yes," she replied. "He died on the twenty-ninth of May in 1790 at the age of seventy-two years. There is an inscription on the marble slab over his grave that says that he was ever tenderly attentive to the lives and happiness of his men and that he dared to lead where any dared to follow. It speaks of how much the country owes to his disinterested and gallant exertions. It speaks of his generosity as singular, his honesty proverbial, and says that he was one who, with small advantages, slender education, and no powerful friends, raised himself to universal esteem, and to offices of eminent distinction by personal worth and the diligent services of a useful life."

CHAPTER EIGHTH

"THANK YOU FOR telling us about Putnam, grandma," said Elsie. "I think he was an American to be proud of. Now, if you are not too tired, won't you tell us the story of Jane McCrea? I know a little of it, and I would like to know more."

"I am willing to tell you the little I know about her," replied Mrs. Travilla in her kindly, pleasant tones. "She was the daughter of a Scotch Presbyterian minister of Jersey City, opposite New York. In that city—New York—lived a family of the name of Campbell. A daughter of theirs and Jennie had become very intimate. Mr. Campbell died at sea, and his widow married a Mr. McNeil. He, too, was lost at sea, and she removed with her family to an estate owned by him at Fort Edward. Jane had a brother living near there. Mr. McCrea, the father, was a widower, and when he died, she went to live with her brother. Being so near the McNeils, the intimacy was renewed, and she spent much of her time in Mrs. McNeil's house. Mrs. Jones, a widow with six sons, also lived near the McCreas, and one of them, named David, became Jennie's love interest. When the war broke out, he and his brothers became Tories, and in the Autumn of 1776, David and his brother Jonathan went to Canada. When Burgoyne collected his forces at St. Johns at the foot of Lake Champlain, David and Jonathan Jones were among them. Jonathan was made a captain and David a lieutenant in the division under General Fraser, and they were with the British army near Sandy Hill. Jennie's brother was a Whig and prepared to remove to Albany, but Mrs. McNeil was a staunch loyalist, a cousin of General Fraser, and intended to remain at Fort Edward. Jennie was at Mrs. McNeil's and lingered there even after it was known that the British were near. Her brother had sent her repeatedly urgent requests to join him where he was—five miles farther down the river and be ready to flee when necessity should compel. But she lingered, probably with the faint hope of seeing her love again. At last, her brother sent a peremptory order for her to join him, and she promised to go down to the spot where he was in a large bateau, which was expected to leave with several families the next day.

"But Jennie had waited too long. Early the next morning, a servant boy belonging to Mrs. McNeil espied some Indians stealthily approaching the house, and, giving the alarm, he fled to the fort about eight rods distant.

"Jennie's young friend, Mrs. McNeil's daughter, was away from home at the time, and the family there just then consisted only of Mrs. McNeil, Jennie, two small children, and a female servant.

"The kitchen stood a few feet from the house, and when the alarm was given, the servant woman snatched up the children, fled with them to the kitchen, and from there, through a trap door, into the cellar.

"Mrs. McNeil and Jennie followed. Jennie, young and able to move briskly, reached the trap door first, but Mrs. McNeil, being old and corpulent, could not move rapidly. Before she could get down into the cellar, the Indians were in the house, and a powerful savage seized her by the hair and dragged her up. Another went into the cellar and brought out Jennie, but the darkness of the cellar favored the colored woman and the children. It would seem the Indians did not see them, and so left them in their hiding place unharmed.

"The Indians started off on the road to Sandy Hill, taking Mrs. McNeil and Jennie with them. That was the road to Burgoyne's camp.

"When they came to the foot of a hill where the road forked, they caught two horses that were grazing and tried to mount their prisoners upon them. Mrs. McNeil was too heavy to be lifted on the horse easily, so told the Indians by signs that she could not ride. Then two stout ones of them took her by the arms and hurried her up the road over the hill, while the others with Jennie on the horse went along the road running west of a tree.

"The boy who ran to the fort gave the alarm, and a small detachment was immediately sent out for the rescue of the captured ones. They fired several volleys at the Indians without hitting them. Lossing, whose version of the sad story I am giving you, goes on to tell that Mrs. McNeil said the Indians who were hurrying her up the hill seemed to watch the flash of the guns and several times threw her upon her face, at the same time falling down themselves. She distinctly heard the balls whistle above them. The firing ceased when they had gotten to the second hill from the village. They stopped there and stripped her of all her garments except her chemise. Then they led her in that plight into the British camp. Her cousin, General Fraser, was there, and she reproached him bitterly for sending his 'scoundrel Indians' after her. He said he did not know of her being away from New York City, and he took every pain to make her comfortable. She was so large that not a woman in the camp had a gown big enough for her, so Fraser lent her his camp coat for a garment and a pocket handkerchief to take the place of her stolen cap.

"Very soon after she was taken into the camp, two parties of Indians came in with fresh scalps, one of which Mrs. McNeil at once recognized by the long glossy hair as that of Jennie McCrea. She was horror struck and boldly charged them with murder of the poor girl. They, however, stoutly denied it. They said that while hurrying her along the road on horseback near the spring west of the pine tree, a bullet intended for them from one of the American guns mortally wounded the poor girl, and she fell from the horse. They had lost a prisoner for whom they expected a reward, and the next best thing was to take her scalp and bear it in triumph to the camp and get the promised reward for such trophies.

"Mrs. McNeil always believed their story to be true, as she knew they had been fired upon by the detachment from the fort, and that it was far more to their interest to take a prisoner to the British camp than a scalp. For they would get the larger price for the former. Burgoyne had told the Indians they should be paid for prisoners whom they took, but they would be called to account for scalps."

"So it seems Burgoyne wasn't all bad then," commented Eric. "And I think it must have been a good deal more trouble to get that big, fat, old woman into the camp alive than it would have been to get the young girl there without killing her."

"Was her lover there in that camp, grandma?" asked Eric.

"No. Lieutenant Jones was not there, but it was known that she was betrothed to him. The story circulated that he had sent the Indians for her, that they quarreled on the way concerning the reward he had offered, and murdered her to settle the dispute.

"The story grew in horror as it passed from one to another and produced a deep and wide-spread indignation. It was increased by a published letter from Gates to Burgoyne charging him with allowing the Indians to butcher with impunity defenseless women and children.

"Burgoyne denied it, declaring that the case of Jane McCrea was the only one act of Indian cruelty he had heard of. That assertion is hard to believe, for the savages murdered a whole family—a man, his wife, three children, a sister-in-law, and three servants near Fort Edward on the same day that Jennie lost her life. They were Tories, but, afraid of the savages, they were getting ready to flee to Albany. On that fatal morning, a young daughter of Mr. Gilmer went to help Mrs. Allen with her preparations to move, and, staying longer than had been expected, her father sent a servant boy down for her. He soon came back screaming, 'They are all dead—father, mother, young missus, and all.' And it was too true. That morning, while they were at breakfast, the Indians had burst in upon them and killed every one."

"What did the Gilmers do about it, grandma?" asked Ned.

"Hurried away to Fort Edward, going very cautiously for fear of meeting Indians. And they did see some of the party who had plundered Mrs. McNeil's house in the morning. They had emptied the straw from the beds and filled the ticks with various things that they had stolen. And Mrs. McNeil's daughter, who was with the Gilmers, saw her mother's looking-glass tied upon the back of one of the Indians."

"And did those folks get safely to Fort Edward, grandma?" asked Ned.

"They did," replied Mrs. Travilla. She then went on with her story. "The story of Jennie McCrea's massacre became known all over the civilized part of this land and in Europe. Burk, says Lossing, used it with powerful effect in the British House of Commons. Burgoyne summoned the Indians to council and demanded the surrender of the one who bore off the scalp of Jennie McCrea to be punished as a murderer. But from policy he pardoned him, lest the Indians should be so offended if he punished him that they would cease to help the British in their efforts to conquer the Americans.

"It had been said that Lieutenant Jones had sent his Jennie a letter by the Indians and them as an escort to take her to the British camp. But he denied it all. Indeed, he had no need to send for her, as the Americans were retreating and leaving only a small guard at Fort Edward. In a day or two the British would have been in full possession of the fort, so that he and his Jennie might have had a safe personal interview."

"Is there anything more known about Lieutenant Jones, grandma?" asked Eric.

"Lossing tells us that he had an interview with some connections of Jones's family and learned that he lived in Canada to be an old man and died there. The death of his Jennie was a dreadful blow to him, and he never recovered from it. He had been merry and very talkative when quite young, but after that sad event he was melancholy and taciturn. He never married and went into society as little as he could without neglecting business. Every year, he kept the anniversary of Jennie's death—he would shut himself in his room and refuse to see any one. His friends felt for him and were careful not to speak of the Revolution in his presence. He bought Jennie's scalp and kept it as one of his most cherished possessions."

"Grandma, was Jennie buried? And if so, is it known where?" asked Elsie.

"Yes, Lossing tells that a picket-guard of one hundred men under Lieutenant Van Vechten was stationed on the hill a little north of the pine tree on that day that we have been talking about. At the moment when the house of Mrs. McNeil was attacked and plundered, and she and Jennie were carried off, other parties of Indians, belonging to the same expedition, came rushing through the woods from different points and fell upon the Americans. Several were killed, and their scalps borne off. The party that went out from the fort in pursuit found their bodies. Jennie and an officer were found lying near together close by the spring only a few feet from the pine tree. They were stripped of clothing. The bodies were carried immediately to the fort—the Americans at once evacuated it—and the body of Jennie was sent down the river in the bateau in which she was to have gone to her brother. It seems that he was very fond of her, and he took charge of her mutilated corpse with the deepest grief. It was buried at the same time and place with that of the lieutenant on the west bank of the Hudson near the mouth of a small creek about three miles below Fort Edward."

"Did the Indians kill Mrs. McNeil, grandma?" asked Ned.

"No. She lived a good many years, and her grave can be seen in the village cemetery near the ruins of the fort. Lossing says that in the summer of 1826, the remains of Jennie were taken up and put in the same grave with her. A plain, white, marble slab with only the name 'Jane McCrea' on it marks the spot."

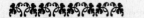

CHAPTER NINTH

THE CHILDREN'S BEDTIME had come, and they had gone to their sleeping quarters for the night. Grandma Elsie was holding the new baby while having a bit of a chat with Evelyn. Most of the other grown people were enjoying themselves together in the parlor, but Lucilla and her father were pacing the front porch, as they so often did, while Mamma Vi put the younger ones to bed.

"Have you had a pleasant time today, daughter?" asked the captain.

"Oh, yes, sir," she replied. "I paid Eva a visit and enjoyed holding and looking at the darling little newcomer — baby Mary. I like the name. Don't you, too, father?"

"Yes, both the name and the one who bears it. What else have you been doing?"

"Sitting out here with a bit of needlework while Grandma Elsie gave us some interesting passages from the history of our country in Revolutionary days — of Putnam and his services, and the sad story of poor Jane McCrea. I have been thinking, father, that you could give us interesting facts concerning other actors in the thrilling scenes and experiences of those dark days for our country."

"Perhaps so," he answered, "though I doubt if I should equal mother as a narrator."

"A doubt I don't in the least share, father," laughed Lucilla. "You always speak the truth, but you are a good story teller for all that."

"That is the judgment of my partial daughter," the captain responded with an amused look and smile. "There are other Revolutionary heroes," he continued, "the facts concerning whom would make very interesting tales — Morgan and Schuyler, for instance."

"And you will tell them to us, father? Oh, that will be fine."

"I shall be very glad indeed if I can add to the information and enjoyment of my own young people and the others," he returned. "Evelyn has quite a library here collected by her father, in which are a number of encyclopedias and historical works — those of Lossing and others. I shall refresh my memory in regard to Morgan and Schuyler and perhaps tell you something of one or both tomorrow evening should Grandma Elsie feel disinclined for such work."

It was settled at the tea table the next day that the captain was to be the narrator for the little company for that evening, Grandma Elsie saying she would greatly prefer being a listener. All gathered about him on the front porch directly upon leaving the table, and he began the story at once.

"Daniel Morgan was born in New Jersey about 1737. There is little or nothing known of his parents except that he had a pious mother and that he was of Welsh extraction. When about seventeen years old, he went to Virginia, where he worked as a farmer for some years. Early in 1754, he moved to Charlestown, Virginia, and the next year he began his military career, going with Braddock's army in the expedition against Fort duQuesne.

"He seems to have been a teamster, and in the rout, he did good service in bringing away the wounded after the defeat. Washington, you will remember, was there as aid-de-camp to Braddock, and doubtless he and Morgan became very well acquainted then.

"It is said that Morgan was unjustly punished with five hundred lashes for knocking down a British officer who had struck him with the flat of his sword.

"After, he was attached to the quartermaster's department, and his duty was to haul supplies to the military posts along the frontier.

"About that same time at the head of some backwoodsmen, he defeated a small force of Frenchmen and Indians and received from Governor Dinwiddie an ensign's commission.

"Afterward, while on his way to Winchester with dispatches, he and others engaged in a fierce woodland fight with the Indians, in which nearly all Morgan's companions were killed, and he was severely wounded, being shot through the neck with a musket ball. At the moment, he supposed the wound would be fatal — he was almost fainting — but resolved not to leave his scalp in the hands of the Indians. He fell forward with his arms tightly clasped about the neck of his horse, and though mists were gathering before his eyes, he spurred away through the forest paths, until his foremost Indian pursuer, finding it impossible to come up with him, hurled his tomahawk after him with a yell of baffled rage and gave up the chase. That was the only wound he ever received."

"And it didn't hinder him from doing great service to his country in the Revolutionary War," remarked Eric Leland.

"Some few years later," continued the captain, "Morgan obtained a grant of land, took to farming and stock raising, and married a farmer's daughter, Abigail Bailey, who is said to have been a woman of rare beauty and lofty character. He named his home the 'Soldier's Rest,' but he was soon called away from it by Pontiac's War. In that, he served as a lieutenant. He prospered with his family and acquired considerable property. But the calls to war were frequent. In 1771, he was commissioned captain of the militia of Frederick County, and two years later he served in Lord Dunmore's war on the frontier."

Chapter Tenth

"In June of 1775, Congress called for ten companies of riflemen from Pennsylvania, Virginia, and Maryland to join the Continental army besieging Boston," continued the captain. "Morgan was chosen captain of one of the Virginia companies, consisting of ninety-six men, and with it he reached Cambridge about the middle of July.

"A month later eleven hundred hardy men were detached from the army for the service of Arnold in his expedition against Canada, and its riflemen were commanded by Captain Daniel Morgan. We will not go over the story now of that toilsome, perilous, and unfortunate expedition. The journey through the wilderness was a terrible one, but our brave men persevered and reached Canada. Morgan and his men were the first to cross the St. Lawrence and reconnoiter the approaches to Quebec, which was too strongly defended to be attacked with any hope of success. But a great attack was made on New Year's morning of 1776, in which Montgomery was killed and Arnold disabled. Morgan stormed the battery opposed to him, but not being supported, he and his detachment were surrounded and taken prisoners. But General Carleton, admiring Morgan for his bravery, released him on parole and he went home to Virginia.

"Washington earnestly recommended him to Congress as worthy of promotion, and in November they gave him a colonel's commission. He was duly exchanged and released from parole. He raised a regiment of riflemen and joined the army at Morristown, New Jersey late in March.

"Morgan's services in reconnoitering were very great in the skillful campaign of the following June, in which Washington prevented Howe from crossing New Jersey.

"In the following July, Burgoyne's descent into northern New York made it desirable to concentrate as large a body of troops there as possible to oppose him, and on the sixteenth of August, Morgan was sent with his regiment to join the army near Stillwater, of which Gates had lately taken command. His force was five hundred picked riflemen, of whom Washington said that he expected the most eminent service from them; nor was he disappointed. And it is said that when Burgoyne was introduced to Morgan after the Battle of Saratoga, he seized him by the hand and exclaimed: 'My dear sir, you command the finest regiment in the world!' It was no wonder that Burgoyne thought highly of their skill—for Morgan and his men had played a principal part in the bloody battle of Freeman's farm, in which Arnold frustrated Burgoyne's attempt to dislodge the American left wing from Bemis Heights. Their services were quite as great in the final conflict of October seventh, in which the British army was wrecked."

"Wasn't it in that Battle of Bemis Heights that General Fraser was killed, papa?" asked Elsie.

"Yes," replied her father. "Morgan's men were skillful riflemen, and one of them shot Fraser.

Morgan, seeing that by directing and cheering on the British troops, Fraser was doing more than any one else to defeat and slay Americans. He perceived that much of the fate of the battle rested upon him and that to bring victory to the Americans, who were fighting for freedom, it was necessary that Fraser should be taken away. So, calling a file of his best men around him, he pointed toward the British right and said, 'That gallant officer is General Fraser. I admire and honor him, but it is necessary that he should die. Victory for the enemy depends upon him. Take your station in that clump of bushes and do your duty.'

"Lossing says, 'Within five minutes, Fraser fell mortally wounded and was carried to the camp by two grenadiers. Shortly before that, two rifle balls had struck very near him, one cutting the crupper of his horse and the other passing through his mane, a little behind his ears. Seeing all that, Fraser's aid begged him to retire from that place. But Fraser replied, 'My duty forbids me to fly from danger,' and the next moment came the shot that killed him."

"Oh, papa, it was a sad, sad thing to do—a sad thing to order!" exclaimed Elsie. "I don't see how Morgan could do it."

"It was a sad thing. War is always dreadful and a great and fearful wrong—often on both sides, sometimes right on one—as I think it was in our War of the Revolution. It was very wicked on the side of King George and his ministers but right and praiseworthy on the part of the Americans who were fighting for freedom for themselves and their posterity. I cannot see why it should be thought any more sinful to kill Fraser than any one of the privates under him, whom he was ordering to shoot our men. No doubt his death at that time saved many—probably hundreds of the lives of Americans who were fighting for life, liberty, home, wives, and children.

"The mortal wounding of Fraser had a good effect—a panic spread along the British line. Burgoyne, who now took the command, could not keep up the sinking courage of his men. The whole line gave way and fled hastily to their camp.

"But I shall not go farther into the account of that battle at present. In the one which followed on the seventh of October, in which the British army was wrecked, Morgan's services were equally great and important.

"After the victory, Gates was unwilling to send Morgan and his regiment back to Washington at Whitemarsh, and it was only with some difficulty and by sending Colonel Hamilton with a special message that the sorely tried commander-in-chief succeeded in obtaining him.

"Washington was at Whitemarsh near Philadelphia, and on the eighteenth of November in 1777, Morgan joined him there in time to take part in the fight early in December of that year.

"On Sunday the eighth, they advanced, and flanking parties were warmly attacked by Colonel Morgan with his rifle corps and Colonel Gist with the Maryland militia. The battle was quite severe. Twenty-seven men in Morgan's corps were killed and wounded beside Major Morris, a brave and gallant officer, who was badly maimed. Sixteen or seventeen of the Maryland militia were wounded.

"The enemy's loss, too, was considerable. The movements of the British seemed to indicate an intention to immediately attack the Americans, so that Washington was presently surprised to perceive that instead of advancing they were marching precipitately, in two divisions, toward Philadelphia. As their adjutant remarked to Mrs. Lydia Darrah, whose story you have all heard before, they had been on a fool's errand and accomplished nothing.

"On the twenty-fifth of August in 1777, Washington with several divisions of his troops, Morgan and his rifle corps among them, left Philadelphia and encamped at Red Clay Creek, a few miles below Wilmington, the next day. Washington established his headquarters at Wilmington and at once made preparations to oppose the march of the enemy, scouts having brought him news of their arrival at the head of Elk.

"In September, Washington broke up his camp and crossed the Brandywine at Chadd's Ford at about two o'clock on the morning of the ninth. The eleventh of September was the day of the Battle of Brandywine."

"Which was a sad defeat for us. Wasn't it, uncle?" asked Eric.

"Yes, though our troops fought very bravely," replied Captain Raymond. "There were about eleven thousand of them, and the British force was probably not less than seventeen thousand men. Lossing tells us that had not conflicting intelligence perplexed and thwarted him in his plans, it is probable that victory would have attended Washington and the American army. He was not dispirited.

"But to go back to Morgan. When in June of 1778, Sir Henry Clinton evacuated Philadelphia and set out for New York by way of New Jersey, the news presently reached Washington, and he at once broke up his encampment at Valley Forge, and with almost his whole army started in pursuit.

"Morgan was in that army with six hundred men. This was on June twentieth. I will not go over the whole story. The battle of Monmouth was not fought until the next Sunday, which was the twenty-eighth and an exceedingly hot day. I shall not go into the particulars in regard to it just now, but only remark that Morgan was most unaccountably kept out of the conflict—he and his brave riflemen at a distance from the field. For hours he was at Richmond Mills, three miles from Monmouth Court House, awaiting orders in an agony of desire to engage in the battle. He was within sound of its fearful tumult. He strode to and fro, uncertain what course to pursue, and, like a hound on a leash, panting to be away to action. It is not known why he was not permitted to take part in that conflict. It seems altogether likely that had he fallen upon the British rear with his fresh troops at the close of the day, Sir Henry Clinton and his army might have shared the fate of Burgoyne and his at Saratoga.

"After the battle, Morgan joined in the pursuit of the enemy and took many prisoners.

"About a year later, finding his health seriously impaired and, like many other officers, feeling much dissatisfaction with the doings of Congress, especially with regard to promotion, Morgan sent in his resignation and went home to Winchester.

"About a year after that, when Gates took command of the southern army, Morgan was urged to return to service. But he refused to serve as a colonel. If he did, he would be outranked by so many commanders of state militia that his movements would be seriously hampered and his usefulness impaired. As Congress declined to promote him, he remained at home, but after the great disaster at Camden, he declared that it was no time to let personal considerations have any weight, and he promptly joined Gates at Hillsborough.

"That was in September. In October, he received promotion, being made a brigadier-general, and Congress soon had reason to rejoice over the fact that it had done that act of justice, since it had resulted in placing Morgan where his great powers could be made of the uttermost service to our country.

"It was in December that Greene took command of the southern army, and he then sent Morgan with nine hundred men to threaten the important inland posts of Augusta and the Ninety-six and to cooperate with the mountain militia. In order to protect those posts and his communication with them, Cornwallis sent the redoubtable Tarleton with eleven hundred men to dispose of Morgan. As they drew near, Morgan retreated to the grazing ground known as the Cowpens, where on a long rising slope, he awaited Tarleton's attack. His men were drawn up in two lines with the militia under Pickens in front and the Continentals under Howard one hundred fifty yards behind. Some distance behind these waited Colonel William Washington with his admirable cavalry.

"When the British attacked Pickens's line, after a brief resistance, the militia broke into two parts and retired behind Howard's line of Continentals. As the British advanced to attack this line, it retreated slowly, so as to give Pickens time to reform his militia. Presently Pickens swept forward in a great semicircle around Howard's right and attacked the British in their left flank. At the same moment, Colonel Washington swept around Howard's left and charged upon the enemy's right flank while Howard's line, after a few deadly volleys at thirty yards, rushed forward with leveled bayonets.

"Thus terribly entrapped, most of the British threw down their arms and surrendered, while the rest scattered and fled. They lost heavily in numbers of killed, wounded, and captured, besides two field pieces and one thousand stand of arms. Only 270 escaped, among them Tarleton, who bravely saved himself in a furious single combat with Colonel Washington.

"The loss of the Americans in this astonishing action was twelve killed and sixty-one wounded. It is said that in point of tacticsm, it was the most brilliant battle of the Revolutionary War. And it is brilliant even compared with the work of the greatest masters of the military art.

"That victory of the Americans was a crippling blow to Cornwallis, because it deprived him of his most effective light infantry.

"Cornwallis was nearer than Morgan to the fords of the Catawba, which Morgan must cross to rejoin Greene. But by a superb march, Morgan gained the river first, crossed it, and kept on into North Carolina.

"There was a masterly series of movements there after Greene's arrival, which ended in the Battle of Guilford and Cornwallis's retreat into Virginia.

"But before the campaign ended, Morgan was suffering so severely with rheumatism that he was compelled to quit active work and go home.

"That was in February of 1781. By the following June, he had so far recovered that he was able to command troops to suppress a dangerous Loyalist insurrection in the Shenandoah Valley.

"Morgan then reported to Lafayette at his headquarters near Jamestown and was out in command of all the light troops and cavalry in the marquis' army. But in August, a return of his rheumatism again obliged him to go home.

"For the next thirteen years, he had a quiet life upon his estate. He grew wealthy and entertained many eminent and interesting guests. His native qualities of mind were such as to make his conversation instructive and charming in spite of the defect of his early education.

"In 1795, with the rank of major-general, he held a command in the large army that, by its mere presence in Western Pennsylvania, put an end to the whiskey insurrection. The next year, he was elected by the Federalists to Congress. But failing health again called him home before the end of his term, and from that time until his death, he seldom left his fireside. He died on the sixth of July in 1802, during the sixty-seventh year of his age."

"Was he a Christian man, papa?" asked Elsie.

"I think he was," her father said in reply. "He had a pious mother, and it seems he never forgot her teachings. In his later years, he became a member of the Presbyterian church in Winchester. 'Ah,' he would often exclaim, when talking of the past, 'people said old Morgan never feared — they thought old Morgan never prayed. They did not know old Morgan was miserably afraid.' He said he trembled at Quebec, and in the gloom of early morning, when approaching the battery at Cape Diamond, he knelt in the snow and prayed. And before the Battle at Cowpens, he went into the woods, ascended a tree, and there poured out his soul in prayer for their protection.

"Morgan was large and strong. He was six feet in height, very muscular, and weighed more than two hundred pounds. His strength and endurance were remarkable, and he was a very handsome man said to be equaled by but few men of his time in beauty of feature and expression. His manners were quiet and refined. His bearing was noble, and his temper sweet, though his wrath was easily aroused by the sight of injustice."

"No wonder, then, that he took up arms against King George," remarked Lucilla.

"A natural result of having such a disposition," returned her father. He went on with his story.

"Morgan was noted for truthfulness and candor, and throughout life, his conduct was regulated by the most rigid code of honor. He was also, as I have said, a devout Christian."

"Oh, I am so glad of that!" exclaimed little Elsie. "I hope we will all meet him in heaven—the dear, brave, good man."

"I hope we will, daughter," responded the captain heartily, while several of his other listeners looked as if they shared the feelings of love and admiration for the brave patriot, Daniel Morgan.

*The author's grandfather, Samuel Finley, had charge of the artillery (one cannon) at the Battle of the Cowpens, was afterward complimented at the head of his regiment, and called, "the brave little major."

CHAPTER ELEVENTH

IT WAS NOW A little past the children's bedtime, so they bade goodnight and went within doors. Gracie and Harold and Mr. Leland withdrew from the porch also, and the captain and Lucilla had it to themselves. They paced back and forth, arm in arm, conversing in rather subdued tones.

"You heard from Chester today?" he inquired.

"Yes, sir, such a bright, cheerful letter. He is very well, prospering with his business, and enjoying himself morning and evenings at Ion, where they are most kindly insistent on entertaining him until my return. He has been out to Sunnyside and reports that everything is in fine order there—indoors and out. He says he will be delighted to see his wife when she returns, but he hopes she will stay in the north until the weather is cooler."

"That is all very satisfactory," said her father. "I am glad you have so kind and affectionate a husband, and I hope to be able to return you to him in a very few weeks."

"I am glad of that, since the return will not separate me, to any great extent, from the dear father who does so much to make my life bright and happy," she said with a sweet and loving smile up into his face. "Oh, father, how much easier and happier life seems to be to us than it was to those poor fellows who fought the battles of the Revolution through such poverty and suffering. It makes my heart ache to read and to think of the bleeding of their bare feet on the snow as they marched over it and to know that they were in rags and sometimes had little or nothing to eat."

"Yes," said her father, "I feel very much as you do about it. I wish I knew they were all Christians, therefore happy in heaven now."

"So do I, father," she sighed, "but it seems to me one of the very dreadful things about war is its sending so many to death with little or no time for preparation and probably in the heat of passion with their foes."

"That is true," he said. "War is a dreadful thing, but the Revolutionary War was right and commendable on the side of our forbears—resisting tyranny as they were. We, as their descendants, are reaping from it the rich fruit of freedom."

"And it is rich fruit!" exclaimed Lucilla in very joyous tones.

> *"Land where my fathers died,*
> *Land of the pilgrim's pride,*
> *From every mountain side*
> *Let Freedom ring."*

"Sounds quite like Fourth of July, sis," laughed a manly voice behind her. Turning, she found Max standing there.

"Will three be as good a company as two?" he asked in the same lively tone in which he had spoken before.

"Better," replied their father, "at least in this instance, and the porch is wide enough for three to walk abreast."

"And it won't hurt Lu to take one of my arms as well as yours, sir," said Max, offering it.

"Well, I will. It isn't every day now that I get the chance," she responded, slipping her hand into it. "Now I think we will have a fine promenade."

"What report can you give of wife and daughter at the present moment, Max?" asked the captain.

"Oh, they are doing fine. Eva says she feels quite well enough to be up and about if that tyrannical doctor didn't forbid it, and our baby is as good as gold and a great deal more valuable," he added with a happy laugh.

"She's prettier than gold this one of her aunts thinks," laughed Lucilla. "And what a treasure she will be to have about Sunnyside, our pretty home."

"Yes, I hope so. It is very good of you to give her such a royal welcome."

"Ah, if only her father could be with us all the time!" sighed Lucilla.

"Perhaps in that case, his companionship might, at times, grow wearisome," laughed Max. "'Blessings brighten as they take their flight,' and perhaps it may be so with brothers and husbands."

"A remark I should advise you not to make in Eva's hearing," she returned in mirthful tones.

"Ah, she would know just how to appreciate it," said Max. Then, turning to their father, "I was much interested in your account of Morgan, sir," he said. "He was a grand man and did a great deal to win the independence of these United

States, now the greatest, grandest country the sun shines upon."

"He did, indeed," the captain said emphatically, "and deserves to be remembered with love and gratitude. He was a very successful leader in those times of our country's sore distress, and he could not have been had not God given him wisdom and skill in answer to prayer. My son, I hope you will follow his example in that."

"Such is my purpose, my dear father, and has been my practice thus far," Max returned with emotion. "Trusting in God it seems to me is the only thing that can enable one to go calmly and composedly to the post of duty when that lies where the messengers of wounds and death are flying thick and fast."

"Yes, I certainly think so," assented the captain. "Washington, our great and successful commander-in-chief, was a man of prayer—raised up, I have no doubt, by a kind Providence for the work that he did. And there were other praying men among our leaders. It was a fearful struggle, but God helped us and enabled us to become the free, strong nation that we are."

"Oh, how thankful we ought to be!" exclaimed Lucilla. "It seems to me it was a very ridiculous idea that this great big country should be governed by that little one away across the ocean, especially as she wanted to be so tyrannical. It is certainly true that 'taxation without representation is tyranny.'"

"Yes," said Max. "An Englishman, arguing with me the other day about it, said it was so small a tax that the colonists were decidedly foolish to make such a fuss and go to war to avoid it. I told him it was the principle of it, which made them so determined. Because if they allowed the English Parliament to impose a small tax without the consent of the colonies, they might—and would be very likely to—go on and levy other and much heavier ones. The colonists were a free-born people and meant to remain free, preferring even death to slavery."

"Yes, indeed!" exclaimed Lucilla. "That last word of yours, Max, reminds me that George III, highly approved of the slave trade and wanted it carried on. It seems as if he was by no means averse to enslaving the whites of this country."

"Quite desirous to do so, even to the setting of the savages to the butchering of women and children," added Max. "But all that being so long in the past, he in his grave, and our liberties secure, it is hardly worth while now to rake up the faults and failings of the poor, crazy, old king."

"His granddaughter has proved a much better and wiser sovereign," said Lucilla. "Women do sometimes do better than men."

"At some times with things not requiring much physical strength, for example," the captain said with a rather amused glance down into his pretty daughter's face.

"Yes, father, it is certainly true that men excel us in physical strength, but is that any reason why women should be paid less for their work and taxed quite as heavily on their property—if they happen to have any?" she concluded with a laugh.

"No, I think not," was his smiling rejoinder. "Ah, what is wrong, I wonder!" as at that instant, the man in charge of the *Dolphin* was seen coming with swift strides up from the wharf toward the house. They stood still, watching him in silence till he drew near enough for speech. Then the captain asked, "What is it, Mr. Bailey?"

"Oh, Captain Raymond, I have a dreadful piece of news for you," was the reply in a tone that spoke of disturbed feeling. "There is news from Buffalo that President McKinley has been shot."

"Shot intentionally? He has been murdered?" asked the captain in tones that spoke astonishment and horror.

"Yes, sir. It was the work of an anarchist of unpronounceable name. If I had my way, anarchists should be promptly expelled from this land and forever excluded from it."

"Is McKinley dead?" asked Max.

"No, but the wound is supposed to be mortal. Noted surgeons are attending him but have hardly a hope of being able to save his life."

"And what have they done with his murderer?" asked Max. "Torn him limb from limb?"

"That's what would have been done by the crowd in building and street if the police hadn't been able to keep them off till they could get him into prison."

"It was what he deserved," said Max hotly and with emotion, "but the police did their duty. Every criminal has a right to trial by judge and jury."

The voices of those on the porch had been somewhat raised by the excitement, attracting the attention of those of the family who were within doors and bringing them out to learn what was going on. There were questions and answers, expressions of grief and horror and queries as to what had and would be done with the assassin, what hope might be entertained of the President's recovery, and should he die, would Roosevelt make a good and competent successor? That last query came from the ladies, and the gentlemen at once expressed the opinion that he would but also hoped that McKinley would be spared and restored to health and strength.

CHAPTER TWELFTH

XTHE NEXT EIGHT DAYS were with the older people at Crag Cottage, as with the rest of the nation, days of anxiety and alternating hope and fear with regard to the dastardly attack upon the President of the United States. After that came the sad news of his death, and there was mourning all over the land. But the mourning mingled with gladness that so good and capable a successor had been provided so that the country seemed in no danger.

Eva was able to sit up now a part of each day, and her baby grew even fairer, beginning to smile and to coo very prettily thought her young mother and aunts—to say nothing of her proud and happy father. Max wanted to see wife and baby safe in their Sunnyside home, and all began to talk merrily of soon starting on their often-made southward trip in the *Dolphin*.

Grandma Elsie, as usual doing all in her power for everyone's welfare and enjoyment, seemed content to go or stay, as did her son Harold and his Gracie. It mattered little to them where they were if only they might be together. The two couples—Captain Raymond and Violet and Mr. and Mrs. Leland—seemed to enjoy themselves and to feel indifferent in regard to the exact time of leaving.

The days passed very pleasantly. There were walks and drives, trips up and down the river in the *Dolphin*, or many hours passed upon the porch if the weather was fine or the parlor if it happened to be stormy. They were spent in cheerful chat, amusing games, or listening to interesting stories from Grandma Elsie or the captain.

And so the days and weeks rolled on until September was gone and October had come in. Then they felt that they must go—the calls from the loved southern homes were so many and so loud and were reechoed by their own hearts. They wanted to go, yet it seemed a trifle saddening to think of leaving this sweet place on the grand, old Hudson River.

The last evening of their stay was lovely and warm for the season, and until the children's bedtime they passed it on the front porch, where they had a view of the river.

A pause in the conversation was broken by a request from Elsie Raymond.

"Papa, won't you tell us about another of the Revolutionary officers?"

"I am willing to do so, daughter, but which shall it be?" the captain asked.

"I should like to hear about General Greene if the rest of the folks here would," she answered, glancing from one to another.

"I think we would all be pleased to hear about him," said Grandma Elsie, "for surely he was next to Washington in bravery, talent for the work at hand, and success in using it."

So the captain began.

"I think he has no superior than Washington in the art and practice of war. He was a native of Rhode Island, the son of Quaker parents, brought up to be industrious and painstaking. He managed to get a good education largely by his own determined efforts in private study of ancient and English history, law, geometry, and moral and political science. He was also fond of reading books about war.

"Some few years before the Revolutionary War, he was chosen a member of the Rhode Island Assembly, and he was one of those who engaged in military exercises as a preparation for the coming struggle with England for the freedom which belonged of right to the people of this land.

"In 1774, he enlisted as private, and in 1775, he was appointed to the command of the Rhode Island contingent of the army at Boston with the rank of brigadier-general. He was with Montgomery and Arnold in their invasion of Canada. He was made a major general in 1775, and he distinguished himself in the battles of Trenton and Princeton.

"He commanded a division at the Battle of the Brandywine and did great service there. It is said that by his skillful movements then and there, he saved the American army from utter destruction. He had part in the Battle of Germantown also, commanding the left wing.

"Soon after the taking of André, Washington sent orders to General Greene to put the left wing of the army near Tappan in motion as soon as possible and march toward King's Ferry. It was midnight when the express reached Greene's quarters. Before dawn, the whole division was upon the march. But I think you are all pretty well acquainted with the story of André, his doings, and consequent end. So, I shall not repeat it here and now."

"But, papa, won't you go a little more into the Battle of the Brandywine?" asked Gracie.

"Certainly, if you wish it," he replied. "Greene's work was very important there. The British army was much stronger than ours—they having eighteen thousand men, while ours were only eleven thousand. Washington had a very strong position at Chadd's and Brinton's Fords. The British hoped to drive him from it in turning his right flank by a circuitous march of eighteen miles up the Lancaster Road and across the forks of the Brandywine toward Birmingham meeting-house. The British were safe in trying to do this, because their force was large enough to enable them to separate the wings of their army with little risk. Cornwallis conducted the movement in an admirable manner, but did not succeed in striking the American flank, because Washington made a new front with his right wing under Sullivan, near Birmingham meeting house, so that Sullivan received the attack on his front.

"A desperate fight ensued, in which the British army, being so superior in numbers to ours, at length succeeded in pushing Sullivan obliquely toward the village of Dilworth. Had they succeeded in completing that movement, it would have cut the American army in two and utterly routed it. But Washington sent a prompt order to General Greene, who commanded the center behind Chadd's Ford. Washington's order was to stop the dangerous gap, and on receiving it, Greene immediately obeyed, marching his troops five miles in twenty-five minutes. Connecting with Sullivan near

Dilworth, he averted the impending destruction of the army. Wayne then had time to withdraw the center and Armstrong the right wing, all in good order, and the whole army was united at Chester in excellent condition."

"It strikes me," remarked Doctor Harold, "that it was hardly a defeat of our troops. The same careless writers have vaguely described the American army as routed at the Battle of the Brandywine. Surely an army cannot at all properly be said to be routed when it is ready to begin to fight again the very next day."

"No," replied the captain, "and the fact that Washington's maneuvering prevented Howe's return to Philadelphia for fifteen days shows that the Americans were not routed. What saved them from that was Greene's memorable double-quick march to Dilworth and his admirable manner of sustaining the fight at that critical point.

"On the twenty-sixth of September, Howe, having eluded Washington on the Schuykill, entered Philadelphia, stationing the bulk of his army in Germantown. On the fourth of October, the Battle of Germantown was fought. Greene, intending to attack the front of the British right wing, was delayed by the difficulties of his route and a mistake of the guide. So, he did not get to the field as early as was planned, and the ground assigned to him was accidentally occupied by Wayne.

"When victory seemed almost gained by the Americans, an unfortunate mishap turned the tide, and General Greene again with wonderful skill covered the retreat.

"In 1778, he was made quartermaster-general, accepting the office at Washington's earnest solicitation but reserving his right to command on the field of battle.

"On the eighteenth of June, the British evacuated Philadelphia and took up their line of march through New Jersey. Hamilton and Greene urged giving them battle, and on the twenty-eighth of June, a general attack was made on Clinton's forces at Monmouth Court House.

"After the battle, Washington marched northward, crossed the Hudson, and encamped in Westchester County, while Clinton continued his retreat to New York.

"Greene, taking no rest, immediately attended to the numerous orders and dispositions required of him as quartermaster-general.

"On the coming of the French fleet, it was decided to make a combined attack upon Newport. Greene wished to take part in it, and in August, he took up his quarters with one division of the army at Tiverton.

"But the French had a variety of mishaps—chief among them the disablement of their fleet by a tremendous gale.

"Soon afterward, Greene went to Philadelphia at Washington's request to tell Congress of the late expedition and the causes of its failure, and there he was received with distinguished consideration.

"The winter of 1780 was one of great suffering to the American troops for the lack of food and proper shelter. Congress seems to have been shamefully neglectful of them.

"Greene did so much for his country during the Revolutionary War that to tell of it all would make my story too long for tonight, but I shall try to give you some of the most interesting items.

"Greene was president of the board convened for André's trial as a spy in connection with Arnold's treason. With tears, Greene signed the decree of the court condemning André to death.

"It has been asserted but not confirmed, that Greene cast a deciding vote in the council against granting André's prayer to be shot instead of hanged. The reason given was that if punished at all, André should receive the punishment meted to spies, according to the laws of war.

"Greene was given the post at West Point after it was left vacant by Arnold's treason. Greene assumed the command early in October of 1780, but the failure of Gates in the southern field caused his recall in August. By common consent, Greene was considered the best man fit to retrieve the fortunes of the southern army.

"Congress empowered Washington to ask Greene to take Gates's late command. Greene accepted the offered post and found a formidable task awaiting him. He took the command at Charlotte on the second of December in 1780. In front of him awaited an army of 3,224 men abundantly clothed and fed, well disciplined, elated with victory, and led by an able general.

"To oppose this force, he had an army of 2,307, of whom 1,482 were present and fit for duty, 547 were absent on command, and 128 were detached on extra service. All these were half fed, scantily clothed, cast down by defeat, and many of them defiant of all discipline. And the entire country was infested with Tories.

"To Greene's bright mind, it was evident that he could not face Cornwallis with such inferior numbers. He resolved to divide his forces, by which means he might secure an abundance of food, keep the enemy within narrow bounds, cut them off from supplies from the upper country, revive the drooping spirits of the inhabitants, threaten the posts and communications of the enemy, and compel him to delay his threatened invasion of North Carolina.

"With the purpose of threatening the British left flank, Morgan was detached with his famous Maryland brigade, and Colonel Washington's light dragoons were to take up a position near the confluence of Pacolet and Broad Rivers.

"With the other divisions, Greene, after a very laborious march through barren country, took post at Hick's Creek on the Peedee, near the South Carolina line.

"Tarleton was hastening forward with his troops, expecting to strike a decisive blow at Morgan, whom it seems he despised, probably deeming him very inferior to himself in both military knowledge and skill.

"He found Morgan, Colonel Washington, and their troops prepared to receive him and his. Then followed the Battle of the Cowpens, the story of which I told you the other day.

"Cornwallis was furious over that defeat, and set out at once in pursuit of Morgan, leaving behind whatever might hinder his movements."

"But he didn't catch him," cried Ned, clapping his hands with a gleeful laugh.

"No," said the captain, "Morgan managed to keep out of his reach, crossed the river first, and kept on into North Carolina.

"But to tell in detail all of Greene's doings down there in the Carolinas and Georgia would make too long a story for tonight.

"On the ninth of February in 1781, Greene, by a most brilliant march, succeeded in bringing together the two divisions of his army at Guilford Court House. He had expected reinforcements from Virginia, but as they had not yet arrived, he decided to retreat toward them and put the broad river Dan between the enemy and himself. In that, he succeeded without loss of men, baggage, or stores.

"Cornwallis had been pursuing him for two hundred miles, but his troops were now weary and discouraged by their fruitless march. He, therefore, prudently retired to Hillsborough.

"However, Greene soon received his sought after reinforcements, and crossing the Dan, he came to battle with Cornwallis at Guilford Court House. The battle was a tactical success for the British, yet the Americans gained a decided strategic advantage. The enemy — too much shattered to go on with the contest — retired to Wilmington, and from there, they moved into Virginia to effect a junction with General Phillips.

"Then Greene at once turned southward with his army. His reason was given in a letter to Washington: 'I am determined to carry the war immediately into South Carolina,' he wrote. 'The enemy will be obliged to follow us, or give up the posts in that state.' If the enemy did follow, it would take the war out of North Carolina, where the inhabitants had suffered great loss from them, and if the enemy left the posts in South Carolina to fall, he would lose far more than he could gain in Virginia.

"In the latter part of April of that year, the American army established itself in a strong position on Hobkirk's Hill near Camden, and on the twenty-fifth, the British under Lord Rawdon attacked it there. It was exactly what Greene had been preparing for.

"The assault ought to have resulted in the total ruin of the British army, but through an accidental misunderstanding of orders, Greene's very best men in the Maryland brigade behaved badly. He was forced to abandon his position. Yet, as usual, he reaped the fruits of victory.

"He sent Marion and Lee to take Fort Watson, and their effort had been a brilliant success, which now obliged Rawdon to abandon Camden and fall back toward Charleston.

"Greene now had everything in his own hands and went on taking fort after fort from the enemy, all the way to the back country of South Carolina and Georgia.

"Now, Greene's army had been moving and fighting for seven months. Of course, they must have been tired. So, he gave them a rest of about six weeks in a secure position in and about the high hills of Santee.

"After that, he met the British army, now under the command of Stuart, in a decisive action at Eutaw Springs.

"In the morning, the British were driven off the field by a superb charge on their left flank, but after retreating some distance in disorder, they rallied in a strong position, protected by a brick house and palisaded garden, and succeeded in remaining there during the afternoon. This happened only because Greene desisted from further attack until the cool of the evening. Thus holding their position merely on sufferance, the British army absurdly claimed a victory. Some careless American writers — who ought to have known better — have repeated the error. Greene foresaw that the British must retreat at night. They did so, and he then renewed his attack. They were chased nearly thirty miles by Marion and Lee, and very many of them were taken prisoners. Of the 2,300 men with whom Stuart had gone into battle, scarcely more than one thousand reached Charleston. There they remained for the next fourteen months shut up under the shelter of their fleet."

"The battle of Eutaw Springs was a great victory for the Americans. Wasn't it, father?" asked Gracie.

"It was, indeed, a decisive and final one," he replied, "at least, so far as the Americans in South Carolina were concerned. Congress testified its appreciation of it by a vote of thanks and a gold medal for Greene."

"What was the exact date of that battle, father?" asked Lucilla.

"Battle of Eutaw Springs? Eighth of September in 1781. On the fourteenth of December in 1782, Greene marched into Charleston at the head of his army, and the next summer, when the army was disbanded, he went home. On his way there, he stopped in Philadelphia and was greeted there by enthusiastic crowds and treated with great consideration by Congress—the men who had come so near depriving the country of his services."

"Was the war over then, papa?" asked Elsie.

"England had not as of that date acknowledged our independence," replied her father. "But they did so on November 30, 1782, when preliminaries of peace were signed. Those were changed into a definite peace on September 3, 1783."

"But is that all the story about General Greene, papa?" asked Ned.

"Not quite," replied his father. "Some two years after the war was over, he moved to a plantation, which the state of Georgia had presented to him—doubtless in acknowledgment of his great services there in ridding them of British tyranny. He is said to have lived there very happily with a good wife and many congenial friends in spite of having, through the dishonesty of an army contractor for whom he had become security, to bear a heavy pecuniary responsibility. He did not live to be old, dying at the age of forty-four from sunstroke."

"What a pity!" exclaimed Elsie. "Had he any children, papa?"

"Yes, two sons and three daughters."

"I think they must have been very proud of their father," she said after a moment's thoughtful silence. "Thank you, papa, for telling us about him. I'd like to know about all my countrymen who have been great and good and useful."

"As we all would," added Lucilla. "We may be thankful that we have a father who is able and kind enough to tell us so much."

"Yes, indeed!" responded Elsie earnestly and with a loving look up into her father's eyes. "I thank him very much, and hope I shall never forget the good history lessons he has given us."

"Now it is time for my birdlings to go to their nests," said Violet, rising and taking Ned's hand. "Bid goodnight to your papa and the rest and we will go at once to bed."

CHAPTER THIRTEENTH

"WOULD YOU ENJOY a little stroll about the grounds before seeking your nest for the night, dearest?" asked Harold of Gracie, speaking so softly that the words reached no ears but hers.

"I think I should — with pleasant company," she added with a twinkle of fun in her eyes as she lifted them to his so full of love and admiration.

"He who gives the invitation will do his best to be that," he returned, offering his arm as they both rose to their feet.

A few minutes later, they were seated in the arbor on the edge of the cliff overlooking the river — the very place where he had first told the story of his love and she had acknowledged its return. Both remembered that now, and the pleasant story was told again.

A little silence then followed, broken presently by Gracie.

"What a lovely scene this is! What a grand, old river! I am always sorry to leave it, though glad, too, to go home to our own place in the sunny South."

"Yes. A winter here would be too cold for my frail patient," said Harold, pressing affectionately the small, white hand he held in his. "For which reason, as well as others, I am glad we have homes in the sunny South. I only wish that you and I might at once make another for ourselves."

"But father won't allow that for several years to come, and as he lets us be together as much as we will, don't you think we ought to try to be content to do as he says about—about the time for marrying?"

"Yes, dearest. I really do try to be content."

"Yonder lies the yacht. She looks lovely in the moonlight. I am so glad that we can go home in her instead of by public conveyances. It is such a restful mode of travel, and we can feel so much at our ease."

"Yes, I highly approve of it, especially for any patient of mine. I hope we are going to have a speedy and pleasant little voyage. But now, dearest, your doctor thinks it would be well for you to go and begin your night's rest, as a suitable preparation for it."

"Yes," she said, rising and taking his arm again, "and it is not hard to say goodnight, since we are to be together again in the morning."

They found the porch deserted except for the captain and Lucilla, who were taking their usual evening promenade.

"Goodnight, father," said Gracie in a lively tone as she approached him. "My doctor orders me off to bed that I may gain strength for tomorrow's arduous journey."

"Ah!" he returned, drawing her to him and giving her a fatherly embrace. "I highly approve of that prescription and hope you may awake in the morning stronger and better in health than ever before."

"Thank you, father, dear. I hope it won't be very long before you send Lu to join me," said Gracie, turning a smiling face toward her sister.

"Oh, I dare say I'll be up there before you get your eyes shut for the night," laughed Lucilla. "As we don't any more sleep in adjoining rooms when at home, I value the privilege of being near you at night while here."

"And it is well for you to be together, so that if one is sick the other can call the doctor," remarked Harold, regarding the two with a pleased and amused smile.

The next morning found all ready and anxious to start upon their short voyage. The yacht was in excellent condition, their trunks were all packed, the cottage in condition to be left in charge of the usual caretaker. So at a reasonably early hour, they were all aboard.

It was a lovely day, warm enough for most of them to be very comfortable on deck while the sun was shining. The older people sat together chatting in a lively way while the children roamed the deck.

At length Elsie Raymond came and sat down beside her father.

"Tired, daughter?" he asked kindly.

"Not so very much, papa, but I think I'd like to hear a naval story. It seems as if it would be suitable while we are here on a vessel, and I feel sure you must know a good many of them."

He laughed a little at that. "Perhaps I do," he said, "and I suppose it is natural for a naval officer's daughter to crave naval stories. Shall I tell you of the fight between the *Wasp* and the *Frolic*—a fight that took place during our last war with England?"

"Oh, yes, papa," she answered eagerly, at the same time beckoning to the other children to come. They understood and hastened to gather about the captain, and he began at once.

"Near the middle of October in 1812—you know we were then at war with England—the American gun sloop *Wasp* with Jacob Jones for captain and a crew of 137 men left the Delaware and sailed southeast to get into the tracks of the West India traders. On the next day, she met a heavy gale, in which she lost her jib-boom and two men who were on it. By the seventeenth, the weather had moderated somewhat, and she discovered several sails, which were part of a fleet of armed merchantmen from Honduras bound for England under the convoy of the British eighteen-gun brig-sloop of war *Frolic* of nineteen guns and 110 men and commanded by Captain Whiyates.

"Those vessels had been dispersed by the gale the *Wasp* had passed through. The *Frolic* had spent the day in repairing damages, and by dark six of her convoy had rejoined her. Four of them mounted from sixteen to eighteen guns each.

"As Jones drew near, he perceived that the British vessel was disposed to fight and was preparing to allow merchantmen to escape during the engagement. He at once put the *Wasp* under short fighting canvas, and he bore down toward the *Frolic*, which had lost her main-yard in the gale. She now lashed her damaged yard on deck, carried very little sail, and hoisted Spanish colors to decoy the stranger and permit her convoy to escape.

"By half-past eleven, the ships were not more than sixty yards apart and began firing—the *Wasp* her port and the *Frolic* her starboard battery. The sea was rolling heavily under a stiff breeze. The *Frolic* fired very rapidly, delivering three broadsides to the *Wasp's* two and both crews cheering loudly. As the ships wallowed through the water abreast of each other, the Americans fired as the engaged side of their ship was going down, aiming at the *Frolic's* hull, while the English fired while on the crest of the sea, their shot going high. The water flew in clouds of spray over both vessels, they rolling so that the muzzles of the guns went under."

"Then they couldn't fire. Could they, uncle?" asked Eric.

"Yes," replied Captain Raymond, "in spite of that, the firing was spirited and well directed. In five minutes, the *Wasp's* main top-mast was shot away. It fell with the main top-sail and lodged so as to make the head-yards unmanageable during the rest of the battle. A few minutes later, her gaff and main top-gallant-mast were shot away, and very soon her condition seemed helpless.

"But the *Frolic* had been still more seriously injured in her hull and lower masts. She had fired from the crest of the wave and the *Wasp* from the trough of the sea, sending her shot through the hull of the *Frolic* with destructive effect. There was a great slaughter among her crew, but the survivors kept on with dogged courage.

"At first, the two vessels ran side by side, but the *Wasp* gradually forged ahead, throwing in her fire from a position in which she herself received little injury.

"At length the bowsprit of the *Frolic* passed in over the quarter-deck of the *Wasp*, forcing her bows up in the wind. This enabled the *Wasp* to throw in a raking broadside with a most destructive effect.

"They were so close together that the Americans struck the *Frolic's* side with their rammers in loading, and they began to rake the British vessel with dreadful effect.

"When the vessels ran foul of each other, the crew of the *Wasp* were greatly excited and could no longer be restrained. With wild shouts, they leaped into the tangled rigging and made their way to the deck of the *Frolic*, carrying dismay to the hearts of its surviving crew. All of those who were able had rushed below to escape the raking fire of the *Wasp*, excepting an old sailor who had kept his place at the wheel during the terrible fight. A few surviving officers were standing on the quarter-deck of the *Frolic* — most of them wounded. They threw down their swords in token of surrender when Lieutenant Biddle, who led the boarding party, pulled down the British flag with his own hands.

"A great part of the *Frolic's* men were killed or wounded; not twenty persons on board had escaped unharmed. It was at a quarter past twelve that Lieutenant Biddle hauled down the British flag — just forty-three minutes after the fight began. Her total loss of men was over ninety, about thirty of whom were killed outright or died of wounds."

"Were there as many killed and wounded on our vessel, the *Wasp*?" asked Edward Leland.

"No," replied the captain, "five of her men were killed, two in her mizzen-top and one in her main top-mast rigging, and five were wounded, chiefly aloft. She, the *Frolic*, had been desperately defended. No men could have fought more bravely than Captain Whinyates and his crew. On the other hand, the Americans had done their work with coolness. The accuracy with which they fired was remarkable, and, as the contest had been mainly one of gunnery, they won the victory. When the two vessels separated, both masts of the *Frolic* fell and tattered sails and broken rigging covered the dead with which her decks were strewn.

"Lieutenant Biddle was given charge of the prize, and the vessels were about parting company when the British ship of war *Poictiers* with her seventy-four guns and Captain Beresford appeared on the scene. Two hours after Jones had won his victory, his crippled vessel and more crippled prize were recaptured by the *Poictiers.*"

"And all those brave men were made prisoners. Weren't they, papa?" sighed Elsie.

"Yes, but they were soon exchanged, and Congress voted them prize money for their capture. They promoted Captain Jones and Lieutenant Biddle. The press lauded Jones. Delaware, his native state, voted him thanks, a sword, and a piece of silver plate. The Corporation of New York City voted him a sword and the freedom of the city. Congress gave him the thanks of the nation and a gold medal and appropriated twenty-five thousand dollars to Jones and his companions as a compensation for the loss of their prize by recapture."

"I'm glad of that," said Elsie with a sigh of great satisfaction. "I'm sure they deserved it."

"There were some stirring songs made to commemorate the *Wasp's* battle with the *Frolic.* Were there not?" asked Grandma Elsie, sitting near.

"Yes, mother," replied the captain. "They were sung everywhere and by boys in the street. I think I can recall a stanza of one given by Lossing in his *Story of the United States Navy.*

"'The foe bravely fought,
but his arms were all broken,

And he fled from his death-wound,
aghast and affrighted;
But the Wasp *darted forward*
her death-doing Sting,
And full on his bosom,
like lightning alighted.
She pierced through his entrails,
she maddened his brain,
And he writhed and he groaned
as if torn with the colic;
And long shall John Bull rue the terrible day
He met the American Wasp *on a* Frolic.'

"Caricature and satire were pressed into the service of history. A caricature entitled 'A *Wasp* on a *Frolic*,' or 'A Sting for John Bull,' was sent out by a Philadelphia publisher."

"Papa, didn't Lieutenant Biddle get any presents for his brave deeds on the *Wasp* against the *Frolic*?" asked Elsie.

"Yes," returned the captain. "He shared in the honors of the victory. The Legislature of Pennsylvania voted him a sword, and leading citizens of Philadelphia presented him with a silver urn appropriately ornamented and inscribed."

The captain paused in his narrative, and there was a moment's silence.

"That was a very nice story, papa. Thank you for telling it," said Elsie.

"Yes, we are all obliged for it, uncle," said Eric.

"And perhaps you would all like another one?" returned the captain inquiringly, glancing around upon them with his pleasant smile.

He was answered with a chorus of expressions of the great pleasure they would all take in listening to another story of naval doings. So he began.

"Just a week after the *Wasp* had won her victory, a still more important one was gained. In the middle of October of 1812, Commodore Rodgers sailed from Boston on a second cruise. His flagship was the *President* with forty-four guns accompanied by the *United States* also with forty-four guns, being commanded by Captain Stephen Decatur and the *Argus*, bearing sixteen guns, Lieutenant-commanding St. Clair. These vessels were soon separated, the *United States* sailing southward and eastward, hoping to intercept British West India men.

"At dawn on the Sunday morning of October twenty-third near the Island of Madeira, the watch at the main-top discovered a sail. There was a stiff breeze and heavy seas at the time. The vessel was an English man-of-war under a heavy press of sail, and Decatur resolved to overtake and fight her.

"His vessel was a good sailer and gained rapidly on the one she was pursuing. Her officers and men were full of enthusiasm, and as their ship drew near the British vessel, they sent up shouts from their deck that were heard on board the vessel they were pursuing. That was before they were near enough to bring guns to bear upon each other.

"At about nine o'clock that morning, Decatur opened a broadside upon the British ship, but his balls fell short. However, he was soon so near that a second broadside from the *United States* took effect. The two vessels were on the same track and now fought desperately with long guns, the distance being so great that cannonades and muskets were of no avail.

"The shot of the *United States* took a fearful toll upon her antagonist, and she presently perceived that the only way to save herself from complete and utter destruction was to come to close quarters with her foe. So when the contest had lasted half an hour, riddled and torn in hull and rigging, she bore up gallantly for close action.

"Very soon her mizzen-mast was cut by a shot of the *United States* and fell overboard. Then shortly after, her main-yard was seen hanging in two pieces. Her main and foretop-masts were gone. Her foremast was tottering, and no colors were seen flying. Her main mast and bowsprit were also badly shattered.

"The *United States* was yet unhurt. Decatur tacked and came up under the lee of the English ship. The commander of that vessel was astounded by the movement, for when the American vessel bore away he supposed she was seriously injured and about to fly. The blaze of her cannon had been so incessant that, seen through the smoke, the English captain thought she was on fire. It seems his crew thought so also, for they gave three cheers. But when the *United States* tacked and came up in a position to do more serious damage, the British commander saw that further resistance was vain. So, he struck his colors and surrendered.

"As the United States crossed the stern of her vanquished foe, Decatur called through his trumpet, 'What is the name of your ship?' 'His Majesty's frigate *Macedonia*,' replied J.S. Carden, her captain."

"Was she a nice ship, papa?" asked Ned.

"She was before the battle—a new ship and a very fine one of her class. She was rated at thirty-six guns, but she carried forty-nine. But in this fight, she was terribly bruised and cut up. Most of her rigging was gone, and all her boats were shattered into uselessness. She had received no less than one hundred round shots in her hull, many of them between wind and water. Of her officers and crew, three hundred in number, many were either killed or wounded."

"What did Captain Decatur do with her, papa?" asked Elsie.

"He gave up his cruise and returned to New England with his prize. He went into the harbor of New London, and Lieutenant Allen took the *Macedonia* into Newport harbor about the same time. Soon afterward, both vessels sailed for the harbor of New York, where the *Macedonia* was first anchored on New Year's Day of 1813. One of that city's newspapers said of her, 'She comes with the compliments of the season from old Neptune.'

"A splendid banquet had just been given in that city to Hull, Decatur, and Jones, and all over the Union, people were sounding their praises."

"And what did the English think about it all?" asked Eric.

"They were filled with disappointment and unpleasant forebodings," replied Captain Raymond. "While all over the United States, the people were filled with exultation and hope."

"Didn't the state legislatures and Congress make those brave and successful commanders some gifts to testify to the gratitude of the people—their countrymen?" asked Lucilla.

"Yes," replied her father. "Legislatures and other bodies gave Decatur thanks and swords. New York gave him the freedom of the city and asked for his portrait for the picture gallery in the City Hall, where it still hangs. Congress thanked him and gave him a gold medal."

"I'd like to see that," said Elsie. "I wonder if the family holds it yet."

"Very likely," said Grandma Elsie. "Such a thing would be apt to be highly prized and kept to go down from generation to generation."

"Ah! Who do we have here?" exclaimed the captain, rising to his feet as at that moment Max drew near with Eva on his arm. "Eva, daughter, I am truly glad that you feel able to join us."

"And I am glad to be able and permitted by the doctor to do so, father," she returned, accepting the seat which he offered.

"Yes, it is high time you were allowed a little liberty," he said, as he and Max seated themselves with her between them. "Ah! Here come my granddaughter," as the nurse approached with the babe in her arms.

"Lay her on my lap, please, nurse," said Eva. "I am quite able to hold her."

"And if you find her in the least burdensome, pass her over to her father," said Max.

The children gathered around, Ned saying, "Now, Brother Max, make her talk."

"I don't want to. I'm too young," came apparently from the baby lips, and all the children laughed.

"It's rude for big folks like you to laugh at a little one like me," she seemed to say in a hurt tone.

"I'm sorry, I don't mean to do it again, though I am your aunt," laughed Elsie.

"Are you? Then you ought to be very good to me," the baby voice seemed to say.

"Yes, and I intend to be," returned Elsie. "I love you because you are a dear, little soul and my little niece—your father and mother being my brother and sister."

"Elsie isn't your only relation here, though," said Alie. "There are a good many of us. I'm one of your cousins, baby Mary."

"And I'm another," said Eric, "and big brother Edward is another, and so is little sister Vi. You have a good many relations."

"I hope to get acquainted with them all after awhile," returned the baby voice, "but I'm tired of talking now."

"Dear me! She gets tired sooner than some other folks," laughed Edward, turning away. "I guess she'll not grow up into a gossip about other folks' matters."

"I hope not," said Eva, "but I see she is going to sleep now. So, no wonder she's tired of talking."

CHAPTER
FOURTEENTH

A VERY GOOD DINNER was served on board the *Dolphin* that day, and on leaving the table, most of her passengers sought the deck again, for it was a lovely evening, warm and clear.

The captain and Violet were sitting side by side on a settee when Elsie came to them with a wistful, inquiring look on her face that made her father think she wanted something.

"What is it, my little daughter?" he asked, drawing her to a seat upon his knee.

"If it wouldn't be too much trouble for you to tell me about the War of 1812, papa, I should be glad to learn more about it," she said.

"It will be no trouble for me to give my dear, little girl as much information as she may crave about it," he answered, patting her cheek affectionately. "But if you think the other children will care to hear what I tell you, you may call them here before I begin."

"Oh, yes, papa, I will," she answered joyously and hastened away in search of them.

Her summons was obeyed by one and all, as if in expectation of a great treat. They gathered about the captain, and he began.

"We are now at peace with England, and the two nations are good friends, as I hope and trust they may be always. But between the Wars of the Revolution and of 1812, this country was badly treated by the other one in more ways than one. To tell you all about it would make much too long a story for tonight. Lossing says of England in 1810 that she had seized and confiscated property of American citizens to an incalculable amount. She had contemptuously disregarded the neutrality of the American territories and the jurisdiction of the American laws within the waters and harbors of the United States. She had at that time impressed from the crews of American merchant vessels peaceably navigating the high seas not less than six thousand mariners who claimed to be citizens of the United States and who were denied all opportunity to verify their claims. I think it was in February of 1811, that a richly laden American vessel bound for France was captured by a British cruiser within thirty miles of New York City. Early in May, a British frigate stopped an American brig only eighteen miles from New York, and a young man, known to be a native of Maine, was taken from her and impressed into the British service. Other such instances had occurred, and often the men thus shamefully robbed of their freedom were most cruelly treated."

"How, papa?" asked Ned. "What would they do to them?"

"For refusing to work for their captors, especially after hearing of the declaration of War in 1812, some American sailors were most cruelly used. Three who had been impressed on board the British vessel *Peacock* refused to fight against their country and demanded to be treated as prisoners of war. They were ordered to the quarter-deck and put in irons. Then they were taken to the gangway, stripped naked, whipped eighteen times, and put to duty.

"When the *Peacock* went into action with the *Hornet*, they asked the captain to be sent below, so that they might not fight against their countrymen. The captain called a midshipman and told him to do his duty, which was to hold a pistol to the head of Thompson and threaten to blow his brains out if he and his companions did not do service."

"How glad they must have been when the *Hornet* took the *Peacock!*" exclaimed Eric.

"Yes, indeed! For they had certainly been very cruelly used by those who had stolen them from American vessels," said the captain. "And there were others who received still more cruel treatment from them — the robbers of the American seamen. It was no wonder that America was roused to attempt a second war with Great Britain in order to stop these dreadful outrages upon her people."

"The navy did a great deal in that war. Didn't it, uncle?" asked Edward.

"Yes," replied the captain. "They were far more successful than the land forces."

"Oh, please tell us some of their doings!" cried several children's voices.

The captain mused a moment, then began.

"I will tell you some of the doings of Commodore Rodgers in his favorite frigate, the *President*. After some unsuccessful efforts to intercept vessels trading between the West Indies and Halifax, St. Johns and Quebec, but finding none, he determined to try his fortunes in the North Sea in search of British merchantmen. But he did not meet with a single vessel until he made the Shetland Islands, and there he found only Danish ships trading to England. His supplies began to fail, and he went to North Bergen, in Norway to replenish his stock. There, he was disappointed, too, for there was a great scarcity of food all over the country, and he could procure nothing but water.

"It seems he knew that a fleet of merchantmen were to sail from Archangel in the middle of July. But just as he expected to make some prizes from among them, he fell in with two British ships of war. Knowing that he was not strong enough to battle with both at once, Rodgers fled, hotly pursued by the enemy. At that season in that northern region, the sun is several degrees above the horizon at midnight. That enabled the vessels to keep up the chase more than eighty hours, during which time they were much nearer the *President* than was at all agreeable to her officers and men."

"Oh, I hope they didn't catch her!" exclaimed little Elsie.

"No," said her father, "she escaped from them. Her stock and provisions had been replenished from two vessels that had been taken before the war vessels had appeared, and now she turned westward to intercept vessels coming out of and going into the Irish Channel.

"In the next six or seven days, Rodgers captured three vessels. Then he thought it best to change his course, as the enemy was in that vicinity with a superior force. He made a complete circuit of Ireland, then he steered his ship for the banks of Newfoundland, near which he made two more captures. From these he learned that two British vessels, the *Bellerophon* and *Hyperion* frigate, were only a few miles from him. However, he did not fall in with them and soon stood for the coast of the United States.

"Toward evening on the twenty-third of September, the *President* fell in with the British armed schooner *Highflyer,* tender to Admiral Warren's flagship *St. Domingo.* She was commanded by Lieutenant Hutchinson and was a fine vessel of her class—a fast sailer. When discovered, she was six or seven miles distant, but by a stratagem, Commodore Rodgers decoyed her alongside and captured her without firing a gun. She did not even discover that the *President* was her enemy until the stratagem had succeeded.

"Before starting upon this cruise, Rodgers had placed in his possession some of the British signals. He had also had some made on board his ship, and now he resolved to try their efficacy. He hoisted an English ensign over the *President.* The *Highflyer* answered by displaying another and at the same time a signal from a masthead.

"To Rodgers's delight, he discovered that he possessed its complement. He then signaled that his vessel was the *Sea Horse,* one of the largest of its class known to be then on the American coast. The *Highflyer* at once bore down, hove to under the stern of the *President,* and received one of Rodgers's lieutenants on board, who was dressed in a British uniform. He bore an order from Rodgers for the commander of the *Highflyer* to send his signal books on board to be altered, for some of the Yankees, it was alleged, had obtained possession of them.

"The unsuspecting lieutenant obeyed, and Rodgers was put in possession of the key to the whole correspondence of the British navy.

"Pretty soon the commodore of the *Highflyer* followed his signal books. He was pleased with everything he saw on board what he believed was the English vessel *Sea Horse* and admired even the scarlet uniform of Rodgers's marines, whom he took for British soldiers. Invited into the cabin, Hutchinson placed in the commodore's hands a bundle of dispatches for Admiral Warren and informed his supposed friend that the main object of the British commander on the British station at that time was the capture or destruction of the *President*, which had been greatly annoying and destroying British commerce and spreading alarm throughout British waters.

"The commodore asked what kind of a man Rodgers was. 'An odd fish and hard to catch,' replied the lieutenant.

"'Sir,' said Rodgers most emphatically, 'do you know what vessel you are on board of?'

"'Why, yes,' he replied, 'on board His Majesty's ship *Sea Horse*.'

"'Then, sir, you labor under a mistake,' said Rodgers. 'You are on board the United States frigate *President*, and I am Commodore Rodgers, at your service.'"

"Oh, how frightened that British man must have been!" exclaimed Elsie. "Wasn't he, papa?"

"I suppose that at first he may have thought all the commodore had been saying was merely a joke," replied her father. "He seemed astounded, and it was difficult to make him believe that he was really on an American vessel. But the band on the

President's quarterdeck was playing *Yankee Doodle,* and over it the American ensign was displayed, while the uniforms of the marines were suddenly changed from red to blue.

"It would seem that Hutchinson might well feel alarmed at finding himself in the hands of Rodgers, for he had been one of the Cockburn's sub-alterns when that marauder plundered and burned Havre de Grace a few months before. It is said that Lieutenant Hutchinson had now in his posses-sion a sword, which he had carried away from Commodore Rodgers's house on that occasion.

"He had been warned by Captain Oliver when receiving instructions as commander of the *Highflyer* to take care not to be outwitted by the Yankees. 'Especially be careful,' said Oliver, 'not to fall into the hands of Commodore Rodgers, for if he comes across you he will hoist you upon his jib-boom and carry you into Boston.'"

"And did he do it, now that he'd got him?" asked Ned.

"No," said Captain Raymond. "Well was it for him that the enemy into whose hands he had fallen was an American. Rodgers treated him with cour-tesy such as is due to a prisoner of war and soon allowed him to go at large on parole."

"And did Commodore Rodgers get back to his own country, papa?" asked Elsie.

"Yes, three days after the capture of the *Highflyer,* he sailed into Newport harbor, having his prize with him as well as her commander and fifty-five other prisoners. He said his cruise had not added much luster to the American navy, but he had rendered his country's signal service by harassing the enemy's commerce and keeping more than twenty vessels in search of him for several weeks. He had captured eleven merchant vessels and 271 prisoners."

"What could he do with so many prisoners, uncle?" asked Eric. "I should hardly think he'd have room for them in his ship."

"All but those he carried into Newport had been paroled and sent home in the captured vessels," replied the captain.

"Did he go out catching British ships again, uncle?" asked Edward.

"Yes, on the fifth of December in 1813, he sailed from Newport on another cruise in the *President*. He expected to fall in with the British squadron, but with a stiff breeze from the Northwest, he got well to sea without falling in with them. The next day, he captured the *Cornet*, which British cruisers had taken from the Americans. Then he sailed southward. He ran down into the Caribbean Sea and cruised there unsuccessfully for awhile, but he finally captured and sunk a British merchant ship. He then sailed for the coast of Florida.

"Going northward, he was off Charleston bar on the eleventh of February. He did not enter it, however, but continued on up the coast, chasing and being chased, dashing through a vigilant British blockading squadron off Sandy Hook. He sailed into New York harbor on the evening of the eighteenth."

"Then New York did him honor. Didn't she, father?" asked Gracie, sitting near and listening to his story.

"Yes," replied the captain. "Many of the citizens did so, and a dinner was given in compliment to him at Tammany Hall. At that dinner, where most of the notables of the city were present, Rodgers gave this toast: 'Peace, if it can be obtained without the sacrifice of national honor or the abandonment of maritime rights. Otherwise, war until peace shall be secured without the sacrifice of either.'"

"A good toast. I like the sentiment expressed," said Gracie. "I think I have read that a good many gentlemen were present there at the dinner."

"Yes, more than three hundred — many of them shipmasters," said the captain. "A toast was given to the commodore, followed by eighteen cheers and a song that some one had written that morning in his honor was sung."

"Papa," said Elsie, "was it right for him to put the name of a British vessel on his and British uniforms on his marines to deceive the British *Highflyer* so they would come to him and be taken prisoners?"

"No, daughter, I do not think it was," replied the captain. "Though, no doubt, the motive of all of them was good — to defend their country and countrymen from robbery and oppression. But it is never right to do evil that good may come. My good mother's teaching was, 'You should die rather than tell a lie, though it were no more than to deny that two and two make four.' But, no doubt, Rodgers thought his maneuvers all right and fair, and they certainly inflicted no wrong upon the enemy."

"Is that all the story there is to tell about him, papa?" asked Ned.

"Just about," replied his father. "His good ship, the *President*, now needed a thorough overhauling, and the Secretary of the Navy offered Commodore Rodgers the command of the *Guerriere*, the ship which Hull took from Dacres and which might be made ready for sea much sooner than the *President*. The commodore went to Philadelphia, where the

Guerriere was being put in order. Finding that she was not nearly so ready as he had supposed, he informed the Secretary that he preferred to retain command of the *President*. But in the meantime, the *President* had been offered to Decatur. Rodgers courteously allowed that commander to take his choice of vessels, and he chose the *President*. Now, my dears, I think we may consider our naval studies ended for tonight."

CHAPTER FIFTEENTH

THE HOMEWARD TRIP of the *Dolphin* was a speedy and successful one. Her passengers, healthy and happy, enjoyed it greatly, yet were rejoiced when she cast anchor one lovely morning in the harbor near their homes. They were wont to leave her to travel the remaining few miles on land.

They had been expected at about that time, and Edward and Zoe Travilla were there to meet them. Grandma Elsie was the first to step ashore, and Edward caught her in his arms with a glad exclamation, "Oh, mother, I am so rejoiced to have you at home again! We can't do without you. We have missed you every day and every hour."

"And I am very, very glad to be here with you all again," she returned, "you among them, Zoe. Ah, Herbert, my son," as at that moment he and Dr. Conly appeared on the scene, "your mother is rejoiced to see you also, looking so bright and well. You, too, Cousin Arthur," giving a hand to him. "Are all the dear ones well?"

"Yes. And, oh, but we are glad to have you home again," both physicians answered. They then turned to welcome all of the other travelers who were stepping ashore.

It was a most affectionate greeting all around, even the little newcomer sharing in it. Then Edward said, "Now, family and friends, we want you all at Ion for the rest of the day. A big enough dinner has been prepared, and every one of you will be as welcome as possible."

"That is certainly very kind and hospitable of you, Ned," said Mrs. Leland, "but I really think we had better take ourselves and our luggage to our homes first and visit you later on a few at a time."

"No, Elsie, dear," he returned, "we have made the plans and preparations and shall feel greatly disappointed if not permitted to carry out our scheme. Come one, come all, and let us have a jolly time together."

Just then, Chester Dinsmore came hurrying toward them, having just learned in his office of the arrival of the vessel. A joyous, affectionate greeting was exchanged between him and Lucilla, his wife, and then he turned to the other returned travelers. Edward renewed his invitation, adding, "I have been out to each one of your homes and seen that they are all in prime order for you but told the caretakers that you were to dine with us at Ion first. Therefore, they will not expect you until evening or somewhere near it."

"You are very kind, indeed, Ned," said Captain Raymond, "and if my wife and the others are willing to accept your advice—your most hospitable invitation—I shall be happy to do so."

"I should like to," said Violet, "but what about the baggage?"

"Those things can all be sent out immediately to our homes and safely entrusted to the caretakers just spoken of," said the captain.

All now accepted Edward's invitation, entered the waiting carriages, and were driven at once along the good and pleasant road to Ion. There they found a gathering of all the relatives in that region—Dr. Conley's family, Calhoun's also, Rose Croly with her husband and children, the Dinsmores from the Oaks, the Laceys from the Laurels, Cousin Ronald and Annis, and Hugh Lilburn with his wife and children. It had now been nearly a year since Captain Raymond and his party had sailed away in the *Dolphin*, and the reunion of so many friends and relatives gave much undisguised pleasure.

It was a large company but with nothing stiff or formal about it. There were many loving embraces and much cheerful, happy, familiar chat, and soon they gathered about the hospitable board to regale themselves with dainty and delicious fare. The meal was enlivened by an interchange suited to the occasion of thoughts, feelings, and experiences. There was a feast of reason and a flow of soul accompanied by no gluttony or gormandizing.

Conversation and many courses kept them long at the table. But at length, they left it and gathered in the parlor. They had not been there long when Laurie and Lily came in, bringing the tee-tees— Elsie and Ned Raymond's little monkeys. They were delighted to see their pets and thought the pleasure was mutual, though the older people had doubts concerning the evidences of pleasure given by the monkeys.

The nurse had had care of Evelyn's baby while the dinner was in progress, but now she brought her in and laid her in her mother's lap so that she should go and take her meal. Several of the cousins gathered about to look at the little one and spoke admiringly of her appearance.

"She is a little beauty," said more than one.

Then a weak, little voice seemed to come from her lips, "Don't make me vain."

"Oh, no, darling. You are too young for that," laughed Grandma Elsie, "as well as too young to talk so wisely and well."

"Yes, ma'am, but my papa helps me," murmured the weak little voice, and everybody looked at Max and laughed.

"What a nice little truth-speaker you are, little niece," said Lucilla, leaning over the babe and softly touching her cheek.

"I want to be that always, auntie," replied the same little voice that had spoken before.

"Oh, what a good little thing you are," laughed Ned. "I'm glad to be your uncle."

"Tell him he's far too young and far too small to be much use as an uncle," said a voice that seemed to come from someone behind the group about the baby.

Instantly, every head was turned to see who the speaker was. But he seemed to be invisible.

"Why, who said that?" exclaimed Ned.

"Oh, I know. It was you, Cousin Ronald."

"Some people are wonderfully wise," said Mr. Lilburn. "But really, now, did that sound like my own voice?"

"Like one of them, I think," laughed Ned. "You seem to have a good many—even more than Max has."

Ned had his tee-tee on his shoulder, and he seemed to put in his own word.

"Is that the way you talk to me, you saucy fellow?" laughed Ned, giving the tee-tee a little shake.

"There!" exclaimed Lily Travilla. "That's the first time he's spoken since we brought him away from Louisiana in the *Dolphin*."

"I can't talk when there's nobody to help me," was the tee-tee's next remark.

"And Cousin Ronald is helping you now. Isn't he?" asked Ned.

"Yes, and he's good help."

Elsie had Tiny on her shoulder, and he put in his word now, "I think it's my turn to talk a little. I'm glad my little mistress has come home, though I've had a good time on the yacht and here with these good folks."

"I'm glad you have had a good time," laughed Elsie, "and I promise you shall have a fine time at Woodburn, my home, where I'll take you presently."

"Will you let me run about the porches and the grass and climb the trees?"

"Yes, indeed, as much as you like, if you won't run away from your home," answered Elsie, hugging her pet.

"Now, if aunts, uncles, and cousins will step aside for a moment, her grandfather would like to have a peep at the baby," said Captain Raymond, coming up behind the group of children.

They all hastily stepped aside, and he leaned over the baby and chirruped to her. She looked into his face and laughed, as if she knew and cared for him.

"Ah, you really seem to already know and apprently highly approve of your grandpa," he said laughingly. "Evelyn, my dear, she is truly a darling—a very pretty little girl."

"So Max and I think, father," returned the happy young mother.

"And so, I think I may say, do we all," said old Mr. Dinsmore. "I should not at all object to counting her among my great-great-grandchildren."

"Nor would we to having you do so, sir," said Max, coloring and smiling with pleasure. He was very proud of his little daughter and glad to have her admired by others.

"I am proud and fond of the little dear, call myself her uncle now, and hope to be really such one of these days," laughed Harold.

"We all hope so," said Max. "We have absolutely no objection to your claiming that relationship at once, Harold."

There had been some small alterations and improvements made to the house and grounds since the *Dolphin* and her passengers started on that winter trip, and presently most of the company went about viewing them with entire satisfaction and approval.

But the sun was now nearing the horizon, and the Woodburn and Sunnyside folk were growing eager to see and rest in their own loved and comfortable homes. The carriages were brought up, the adieus said, and they went on their way rejoicing. Each family went to its own dwelling at first, but they would not be long apart. That evening would see them all gathered, first at one residence, then at the other, and there would never be a day that would not be spent more or less in each other's society. This would be true of all excepting Max, who must soon return to his ship. The thought of that was all that marred the happiness of that evening with its joyful return to their own loved homes. But Evelyn and all of them tried to put away remembrance of it for the present.

CHAPTER SIXTEENTH

"Home, sweet home!" exclaimed Lucilla, as their carriage turned into the driveway on that first evening after the *Dolphin* had come into port. "Home, sweet home! There really is no place like home."

"Except Woodburn, our dear old home," returned Max in jesting tone.

"No, Woodburn and Sunnyside—so very close together and their inhabitants so nearly related—seem to make but one home to me."

"And to all of us, I think," said Evelyn.

"And you are right, I am sure," said Chester, as the carriage drew up before the entrance. "Ah, here we are at the very threshold of our Sunnyside! Wife, brother, and sister, a glad welcome home to you all." With the last word, he threw open the carriage door, sprang out upon the veranda steps, turned, and helped Lucilla to alight. Max, his wife, and baby followed.

A joyous welcome was given them by all the waiting servants, and each couple moved into their part of the commodious and beautiful dwelling.

"Welcome home, my darling," said Max to his wife. "Welcome home, baby dear," taking the infant in his arms as he spoke. "Oh, Eva, my love, how rich we are with her added to all our other lesser blessings!"

"Indeed, we are! She is a great blessing," said Eva, caressing the child her husband held in his arms. "To me she seems more than all others taken together — except her father," she added, smiling up into his face.

"And to me she is the next one to her mother," responded Max, bestowing a very loverlike caress upon his wife as she stood close to his side. "How good my father has been to provide us with this lovely home so near to his that we seem to belong to his family still."

"Yes," she said with emotion. "And what a dear father he is! I am so glad and thankful that he seems to look upon me as his very own daughter. I had been so hungry for a father after my own was taken to that better land."

"Yes, dearest, I think I can understand that hunger, though I have been spared the sad experience of losing a father," replied Max, his tone speaking even more sympathy than his words.

"And, oh," he added, "I want my little wife to be the most blessed, happy woman in the world."

"I ought to be, and I think I am when my husband is with me," she returned with a smile of love and joy. "What is it Kitty?" as a servant came in, looking as if she had some pleasant news to impart.

"Why, missus, dere's sumfin' jus' come over from Woodburn. De cap'n, he sends it for de baby," replied the woman, grinning broadly as she spoke.

"Ah, is that so?" asked Max. "What is it?"

"Sumfin' for de baby to ride in, sah, an' it's out on de poach," she answered, hurriedly leading the way. Eva and Max followed — he with the baby still in his arms.

They presently found on the front veranda as handsome a baby carriage as either of them had ever seen, and they were both delighted with it. It was ready furnished with pillows and a beautiful afghan of a most delicate shade of baby-blue silk lined with white silk covered with white duchess lace with blue ribbon bows on each corner to match the umbrella, as it was of the same shade and also covered with duchess lace. On the corner of the afghan was pinned a bit of paper bearing the words: "From Grandmamma Vi to little Mary Raymond." On the underside of the afghan were the initials "M. R." in blue embroidery silk.

Max laid the baby in, and Evelyn covered her carefully with the afghan. For some minutes, Max drew her back and forth on the veranda, she cooing as if enjoying the ride.

Chester and Lucilla had quite a good deal to tell each other of their experiences during the past few weeks of separation, and they were chatting and laughing merrily in her pretty boudoir. Some slight sounds made by the baby, her parents, and the carriage excited their curiosity and brought them hurrying downstairs to learn what was going on there.

"Oh, how pretty!" cried Lucilla, as she caught sight of the little vehicle. "How fine for our darling baby! Where did it come from?"

"It is father and Mamma Vi's gift," answered Max, "the dear, kind parents who are always thinking of everything they can possibly do to add to our happiness."

"They do, indeed!" exclaimed Evelyn. "Nobody could have better."

"We are all going over to Woodburn later this evening," said Max, "and we will take baby in her new carriage."

"She, as queen of the party, will ride, and the rest of us will walk," laughed Lucilla. "Oh, you little darling, auntie hopes you will always be able to ride when you want to."

"Doubtless she will if it is best for her," said Max. "It looks now as if she were born for easy times, but no one can tell what may be in store for either us or her in the future."

"Father would say, 'Don't allow yourself to be troubled with anxiety in regard to the future. Remember the teaching of the thirty-seventh Psalm, "Trust in the Lord, and do good; so shalt thou dwell in the land, and verily thou shalt be fed."'" said Lucilla.

"Yes," agreed Evelyn, "if we all had perfect trust in Him, I am sure we should be free from anxiety and very happy."

"I am sure you are right about that," said Chester, "and if we practice it—that teaching—we shall be a happy set."

"I hear our call to supper," said Lucilla. "Eva, won't you and Max come in and sup with us?"

"Do, friends and relatives. We will be very glad to have you partake with us," said Chester.

"Thank you both," said Max. "I think our supper is just about ready, but if you will allow dishes to be added to yours, we may share with each other and probably enjoy doing so."

All agreed that that was a good idea, and the plan was immediately carried out.

The Sunnyside folks were not more glad to see their home than were the Woodburn people to reach theirs. The captain's carriage contained, not his own family only, but his future son-in-law also. Harold was bidding an affectionate good-bye to Gracie on the veranda at Ion when her father said laughingly, "Don't indulge in adieus just here and now, Harold, but come with us to Woodburn. Who can tell but there may be a patient there longing for a sight of Dr. Harold Travilla's face?"

"Thank you, captain for the kind invitation and for flattering my medical and surgical skill and supposed desire to be helpful to others. But I should be sorry to crowd you."

He and her father were helping Gracie into the vehicle as he spoke.

"There's an abundance of room, Harold," said Violet. "Get right in and take that seat there beside Gracie."

"Yes, obey that sweet lady's orders as I do," laughed the captain.

"I thought I had outgrown that business," laughed Harold, "but I will obey in a moment. I must say goodnight to mother and the rest."

That did not take long, and the captain's kind comment of, "Plenty of time for that" seemed to afford satisfactory permission. In five minutes, the carriage was on its way down the avenue.

"Now, Tiny, you are on your way to that pretty home I've been telling you about," said Elsie, stroking and patting her little pet monkey.

"What are you telling her for, Elsie?" asked Ned. "Why don't you wait and let him be surprised when he gets there? Surprises are nice. I always like to be surprised."

"Something of a mistake, Ned," said his uncle. "Some surprises are far from agreeable."

"What kind, uncle? Please tell me about some."

"Well, I have heard of it happening to a man to learn that all of a sudden he had lost all his money."

"Oh, that's not so bad. He could earn more."

"Maybe he could, but if so, he'd a good deal rather add that to what he had before than have only that."

"There must be a good many kinds of surprises," returned the little fellow thoughtfully, "and I'd rather have some other kind than that. When papa gave me my pony, that was a very pleasant surprise. Oh, I was just delighted."

"And these tee-tees were a very, very agreeable surprise to both of us," said Elsie, patting and stroking hers, as he was seated in her lap.

"And I'm thinking Eva and Max will soon have a very agreeable surprise," said Gracie, smiling up into her father's face.

"I hope so," he said, returning the smile.

"Oh, what about?" queried Ned with tone and look of curiosity and excitement.

"No doubt you will learn when they — your brothers and sisters — come over to Woodburn this evening," answered his father.

"Will I?" cried Ned. "Oh, I hope they'll come early — at least, before Elsie and I have to go to bed."

At that everybody laughed, and his mother remarked that she was surprised to find him exhibiting so much curiosity, as it seemed to be understood that that quality belonged rather to women and girls than to men and boys.

"Quite a mistake and slander, my dear," laughed her husband. He then changed the subject of conversation by calling attention to a new building going up on a neighboring plantation.

A few minutes later their carriage turned into the Woodburn driveway, and presently they were leaving it for the veranda of the spacious dwelling where the servants were assembled with Christine, their ladylike housekeeper, at their head to welcome the returned travelers to their home. Everybody seemed full of joy over their return, and the children were delighted with the curiosity shown in regard to their new pets and the to-do made over them.

A bountiful and most appetizing repast had been prepared for their reception, and they presently seated themselves about the table. A blessing was asked, and the captain began carving a fine turkey, Violet pouring the tea. The table was charmingly furnished with beautiful china, cut glass, silver, flowers, and dishes of the most appetizing-looking food.

"It is really very pleasant to be at home and at one's own table again," remarked the captain after an appreciative glance over the board.

"Whose table was it that you sat down to on the *Dolphin*?" laughed Violet.

"My own, I believe," smiled the captain. "But somehow, I feel even more at home here."

"It is delightful to be here, but I do miss Lu," sighed Gracie.

"Well, daughter, she is not far off. Keep up your spirits. She will probably be here in the course of an hour."

"Husband, brother, sister, baby, and all with her, I presume," added Harold sportively. "And baby will probably come in her own coach, like the grand lady she is," laughed Violet. "I shall enjoy seeing her in it."

"Resting on and also covered by the beautiful furnishings provided by your generosity and taste, mamma," said Gracie with a loving, appreciative look at her young stepmother.

"Are we going to have a grand party tonight?" asked Ned.

"Not exactly," said his father, "at least, it will be only a home party of what I call our own immediate family — my children and grandchild."

"Many thanks, my dear captain, that I seem to be included in the number forming that happy family," said Harold with a bow and pleased smile.

"Yes," laughed Violet, "but don't imagine that I am going to permit you to call me mamma, considering that you are my younger brother."

"So I am, Mrs. Raymond, but by no means young enough to be an obedient son to you," returned Harold in playful tone, "or, indeed, any son at all. It will be well enough to bear that relationship to your husband, but it is fairly ludicrous to pretend to bear it to so young and fair a lady as yourself."

"I should think the fairness would make it a trifle less objectionable, if anything could," returned Violet with mischievous look and smile.

"Really, those mutual relationships make small difference, except as they may affect your docility when you are the patient and I am the physician," returned Harold gravely.

"All of us obey your orders when you are the doctor," remarked Elsie. "Sister Gracie will never do a thing that you tell her not to."

"Of course not," laughed Gracie. "What would be the use of employing a physician, if you didn't follow his directions?"

At the conclusion of the meal, all repaired to the veranda to await the coming of the Sunnyside folks. It was a warm October evening, the grounds looking beautiful in their autumn robes, and there seemed no pleasanter place to relax than that with its abundance of most comfortable settees and chairs.

"It is very nice to be at home again," said Gracie with a happy sigh. "I wouldn't be willing to give up this dear home for any of the beautiful places I have been in."

"I am glad you are so well satisfied, daughter," the captain responded in a pleased tone, "and I hope you will never have less love for your father's house than you do now."

"Oh, good, good! Here they all come now!" cried Ned, springing to his feet and clapping his hands as the little group was seen approaching from the direction of Sunnyside.

"Yes, children and grandchild," said the captain, as he and Harold hurried to meet them.

"Many, many thanks, father, for this beautiful and useful gift to our baby daughter," said Max almost before they had fairly met.

"And not from baby's father only but from her mother also," said Evelyn. "Many, many thanks to you and Mamma Vi for both the carriage and its lovely furnishings."

"Ah, those last are gifts especially from my wife," returned the captain.

"Yes, oh yes, I know and appreciate it, but, no doubt, they were given with your approval. Ah, Mamma Vi," as Violet approached, "I hardly know how to thank you enough for your lovely gifts to our baby daughter."

"Then don't try," returned Violet in mirthful tones. "I assure you, the pleasure I found in doing it was reward enough. How is the little dear this evening? Ah, I see she is sound asleep. How nicely her papa must have rolled the little coach along to get her in that condition."

"She does more sleeping than anything else so far in her life," laughed Max, looking down admiringly into the sweet, fair baby face resting so quietly on the soft pillow.

The children, following their parents, had met them now.

"Oh, we want to see the dear baby!" they said in excited but rather hushed voices. "Let us look at her, Max."

"Not yet," he answered. "Let us keep her asleep as long as we can. Then when she wakes by herself she will probably be in a pleasant mood. I don't like to hear a baby cry. Do you?"

They had reached the house, and the gentlemen lifted the coach up onto the veranda without awakening the young sleeper.

Lucilla was on the veranda, gazing about from side to side.

"Oh, how sweet the dear old home does look!" she cried. "I want to go all over this story and the next just now. May I, father?"

"Certainly, my child. It is your own home now quite as much as it ever was. Because you are as much as ever my own dear daughter."

"Thank you for those kind, loving words, father dear," she returned with emotion, laying a hand on his shoulder as she stood at his side and giving him a look of ardent affection.

At that he bent his head and kissed her fondly on the forehead and cheeks.

"It is my turn now, papa," said Gracie sportively, coming up to his other side.

"So it is, my darling," he returned, repeating for her exactly what he had done to Lucilla.

Elsie had noted it all with interest.

"Now, papa, isn't it my turn?" she asked, her eyes shining and her lips curling with a smile of filial love and entreaty.

"Yes, little daughter. Yes, indeed! You are no less dear than your older sisters. Come and give and take the caresses papa loves to exchange with you."

Violet and Evelyn preferred to keep watch over the sleeping babe, but all the others joined in making the circuit of the rooms Lucilla had expressed a desire to see. They found them all in good order, Christine being an excellent housekeeper and having good and competent servants under her.

"It is delightful to come home to houses so well ordered and neat as this and Sunnyside have proved on this occasion, Mamma Vi," Lucilla remarked on her return to the veranda.

"Yes, and I think I fully appreciate it," replied Violet. "You found yours in good order?"

"Perfect. It could not have looked better if I had been there to oversee the work."

"And I can say just the same of mine portion of Sunnyside," said Evelyn.

CHAPTER
SEVENTEENTH

OVER AT ION, the family there was left alone, all the guests having now departed to their own homes. Zoe was seeing her children to their nests for the night. Grandpa and Grandma Dinsmore were chatting together on the front veranda, while Grandma Elsie and her sons, Edward and Herbert, a little removed from the older couple, were engaged in a similar manner. Her sons were asking questions in regard to their mother's experiences during the summer and fall, and she was telling a pleasant and interesting tale in regard to them.

Just then a hack came rolling up the avenue.

"Who's that now, I wonder," growled Edward, "coming to interrupt our first private chat with our long absent mother?"

"Probably somebody wanting the doctor," sighed Herbert, rising and moving toward the entrance.

At that moment, the vehicle came to a standstill at the veranda steps, and instantly out sprang a manly form, who came quickly up them.

"Walter!" exclaimed Herbert, reaching out his hand, which the other grasped and shook heartily.

"Yes, brother mine, it is I. Where's mother? Mother, mother dear! Oh, how glad I am to have you in my arms once more!" as she sprang forward with a cry of joy.

"Walter, my dear, dear youngest son!" and he caught her in his arms. "My baby boy," she laughed in the next moment, "my baby boy grown taller than his mother. Oh, why wasn't he here to meet and greet me when I got home?"

"A little business matter, and a misunderstanding as to the probable time of my mother's arrival," he answered, repeating his caresses.

Then they released each other, and joyous and affectionate greetings were exchanged with the remaining members of the family.

"You should have been here sooner, Walter," said Herbert when all were seated again with his mother in the midst. "She has been telling Ed and me some very interesting things about her recent visit to California."

"Perhaps mother will repeat her story to me one of these days," said Walter. "At present, it seems almost enough to see her dear face without hearing anything but the sound of her sweet voice."

"That sounds very much as if my youngest son had been busy kissing the blarney stone," laughed his mother.

"Not a bit of it, mother," he returned. "You know I wasn't brought up to do such things."

"I hope you were not," she said, "but you have been under other teachers than your mother for some years past."

"True, my mother dear, but I hope I have not forgotten your teachings. Now, what is the latest news about uncles, aunts, cousins, and friends in the neighborhood?"

"I really think but little has taken place that would be new to you, Walter," replied his mother.

"I doubt," laughed Edward, "if he has heard of the good fortune of Eva and Max."

"Money or estate?" queried Walter.

"Something better than either," remarked his mother with a pleased smile.

"Oh, I suppose Max has been promoted. Good for him! He's very happy over it, I dare say."

"But it isn't that. You're wide of the mark," laughed Edward.

"You may as well tell me. I don't seem to be Yankee enough to be good at guessing."

"A little daughter—as pretty a baby as ever was seen, of course, excepting Zoe's and mine."

"Oh, is that it?" laughed Walter. "Well, I'll congratulate them when I see them. Am I uncle to her, mother?"

"No," she replied with a smile, "you are not really related at all to either parent—so, of course, not to the child."

"Yet both the parents and I have been in the habit of calling each other cousin, so I think I'll claim kin to the little beauty you tell me of."

"And I don't think any one will object," replied his mother.

Zoe now joined them, welcomed Walter heartily, and the talk went on, principally about the various relatives and connections but with never an unkind or uncharitable word in regard to any of them.

"You had them all here today," Walter said. "I wish I had reached home a few hours sooner."

"We would have been glad to see you then, as we are now, my son," said his mother. "But don't feel too much disappointed. I have an idea that there will be a number of other family gatherings before Max is ordered away again."

"Yes," said Grandma Dinsmore, "I heard several of today's guests express an intention to have such a family gathering themselves before long."

"And they are the most agreeable kind to have," said Zoe.

"I think I shall go tomorrow and have a peep at the new relative, as well as a chat with her parents," said Walter. "I dare say they must feel quite rich. But how funny to think of the captain and Vi as grandpa and grandma. But, of course, Vi isn't old enough to be that, and nobody would think of calling her so."

"She calls herself that," said Zoe, "but certainly it seems quite ridiculous. They will all be sorry, as we are, that you were not here today to take part in our reception," she added. "But if you would like to speak to any of them now, you know you can use the telephone."

"Thanks," returned Walter, "but I believe I should prefer to give them a rousing surprise tomorrow by just walking in on them."

"I think that the better plan," commented his grandfather approvingly.

"And perhaps I can persuade my mother to go along," added Walter, looking smilingly at her.

"If you get Herbert or Harold to prescribe the ride—or walk. Which is it to be? I will go, expecting a health benefit from so doing," she responded in mirthful tone.

"Harold!" exclaimed Walter. "By the way, where is he? Visiting some desperately sick patient? I know that's often the case when he fails to adorn the family circle."

"No," said Herbert, "at present he is dancing attendance on Gracie Raymond, his much adored and honored ladylove."

Walter laughed and said, "Ah, yes, that's all right. Gracie is a dear, sweet girl—a beauty, too. Except for the odd mixing up of relationships and the fact that she is delicate, I should be delighted with the prospective match."

"I also," said his mother. "I am very fond of Gracie. I have loved her ever since my first sight of her sweet face. I can see that she loves Harold dearly yet is perfectly submissive to her father's will in regard to the time of their marriage. Nor does Harold rebel, though it is plain to see that he longs for the time when he may claim her as his very own."

"Yes, mother. Well, I hope he will prescribe early retirement for his ladylove tonight and hasten home to greet his youngest brother, whom he has not seen for nearly a year."

"I presume he has done so, for here he comes now walking up the avenue," exclaimed Herbert, glancing in that direction.

At that, Walter sprang to his feet and hastened forward to meet Harold as he came bounding up the veranda steps.

"Howdy'do, doctor?" he cried with a pleasant laugh. "I hope you've left that pretty patient of yours doing well."

"Why, Walter, my man, I'm glad to see and know that, young as you are, you've traveled home safely by yourself," responded Harold, reaching the top step and grasping heartily the hand held out to him.

"How do you know that I traveled by myself?" laughed Walter. "Are you quite sure I may not have a ladylove and future father-in-law as well as yourself, Harold?"

"Yes, my little man. For if you had, I should most certainly have learned it before this, since my youngest brother has always been communicative to me."

"Don't be too sure of that, laddie," laughed Walter. "But come along now and join the family circle, which, with you in it, will be quite complete."

"So you are here again, Harold," commented his grandfather, as they seated themselves. "How did you and the Raymonds find matters at Woodburn?"

"Everything is in perfect order, sir—at least, so far as I could tell, and all seemed entirely satisfied and full of delight that they had at last reached their own home."

"That is pleasant news. I suppose you didn't go on to Sunnyside?"

"No, sir. I have reserved that pleasant visit for tomorrow morning."

"Oh," said Walter, "Chester and Lu, Max and Eva are at home now, I suppose. I'm told the latter couple rejoice in having a beauty of a baby."

"Yes, she is a beauty, I think," said Harold, "as sweet a little creature as ever I saw."

"That's pretty strong, coming from an old bach. Isn't it?" laughed Walter.

"Hardly at an age to be reasonably called old, Walter," remonstrated their mother gently and with a smile.

"It seems quite well, from a business point of view, for a doctor to be considered old — or at least not very young, mother," said Harold pleasantly and with a smile.

"Most people are more ready to trust themselves and dear ones to the treatment of a physician who has had some experience in the practice of his profession than to one whose youth proves him to be but a beginner."

"Quite true, Harold, and it is very sensible in those who act upon that very principal," remarked his grandfather.

CHAPTER
EIGHTEENTH

"IT IS A LOVELY morning, one of October's fairest days!" exclaimed Lucilla, glancing from the window of her dressing room on the day after their homecoming from their recent sojourn upon the banks of the Hudson. "Oh, Chester, my dear, I wish you could just stay at home and spend the day with me!"

"It would be very pleasant to do so, my love," he returned, "but business forbids. Besides," he added laughingly, "I feel very sure you would not be content to really stay at home all day."

"No," she returned in mirthful tone, "but Woodburn seems to me only a part of my home—holding my dear father and the other loved ones—and I cannot be content to refrain from spending a part of every day with them or from having them spend a part here with me."

"Yes, dearest, I fully understand, and I rejoice that you have their loved companionship when I must be away from home. You might be very lonely indeed without them," returned Chester. He came close to her side and put an arm about her as he spoke.

"My dear husband," she murmured low and softly, "your companionship has become more and sweeter to me than any or all other, even that of my dear father."

"Oh, thank you for those sweet words, dearest," he returned with emotion. "Ah, I esteem myself a very fortunate man in having such a wife. But it grows late, and I must hasten with my preparations, for breakfast first and business after."

"Do, my dear. I am just ready to go down, and I think the call to breakfast will soon follow my entrance into the dining room."

She met Max in the hall, and they exchanged a pleasant morning greeting.

"How are wife and baby?" she asked.

"They seem to be well, bright, and happy."

"And you are looking so."

"Look as I feel, then, when I can refrain from thinking of Uncle Sam's coming orders," he returned with a rather rueful smile.

"Oh, dear! I'd break loose from that old uncle if I were you. Won't you and Eva come in and take breakfast with us?"

"No, thank you. We were with you last night, you know. So it's your turn to come to us. Take your breakfast with us this morning, you and Chester. Won't you?"

"Thank you, but Chester is so hurried in the mornings. I think he would prefer to join you at tea one of these evenings."

"Ah, yes, that will be better. And there! Both breakfast bells are ringing."

Those sounds brought both Evelyn and Chester into the hall. Morning greetings were exchanged with them, and the four at once descended to their breakfast rooms.

Chester did not linger over his breakfast, but Max and Eva ate leisurely, as there was no necessity for haste with either of them at that time.

Lucilla saw her husband on his way, returned to the table, finished her breakfast, had a pleasant little stroll about the grounds with her father, and returned to the house and found Max, Evelyn, and the baby on the veranda, for it was a bright, warm morning. Eva sat with the babe in her arms, Max standing by her side, gazing in the direction of Woodburn.

"Why didn't father come in?" he asked, his tone expressing disappointment and chagrin.

"He said it was a little too late. Mamma Vi would be ready for her breakfast, and he could not think of keeping her waiting. But he thinks they will be here in an hour or so and convoy us all over there."

"All right, as father's plans always are," returned Max with a sigh of satisfaction.

"Just as I think," said Evelyn, "but I doubt if we can make a lengthened stay, as I overheard occasional remarks yesterday at Ion indicating that we would be likely to receive a number of calls from relatives and friends today."

"But," laughed Lucilla, "they will be calling upon the Woodburn folks, too, and it will be to them a saving of time and trouble to find us all in one house. Will it not?"

"So it will," responded Max in laughing tone, "and I hope they will appreciate our kindness in so evidently consulting their convenience in regard to the matter."

"Ah, how sweet our little darling looks this fine morning!" exclaimed Lucilla, stepping to Evelyn's side and bending over the little one. "Precious pet, Aunt Lu loves to look at you."

"Tell Aunt Lu you will look much sweeter when you have had your bath and are dressed for the day," said Evelyn.

Suddenly, the child seemed to answer, "Let me have it soon, mamma, before my dear grandpa sees me."

"Yes, so you shall," Eva replied with a laughing look at her husband. "Baby dear, you should appreciate the blessing of having a father who can talk for you until you can do it for yourself. Now," she added, rising with the child I her arms, "we will go and make the contemplated improvements."

"And I to attend to household affairs," added Lucilla, and they passed into the entrance hall together to see to their respective tasks.

The families at Woodburn and Ion sat down to their breakfast at very nearly the same time. At both places, all were well and in good spirits, and as a consequence, the chat was lively and pleasant.

"What a lovely morning," remarked Mrs. Dinsmore. "This is certainly to be one of our delicious October days."

"Yes, and quite a good deal of it would be properly spent in walking and driving," said her husband. "Shall I take you and Elsie over to Woodburn and Sunnyside?"

"You may take me any way that suits you best," she returned with a pleased smile.

"And you, Elsie?" he asked.

"Thank you, father," she said, her tone and look indicating a grateful appreciation of his kindness in giving the invitation. "Last evening, I accepted an invitation from Walter, but we might make up a family party and all go. 'The more the merrier,' as I am sure the Woodburn folk would think."

"Oh, do, do! Let us all go!" cried little Lily. "I want to see the monkeys again."

At that everybody laughed, and Grandpa Dinsmore said, "Very well, you can visit the monkeys and the rest of us our relatives."

Lily hung her head and blushed.

"I didn't mean I cared more about the monkeys than about our aunt and uncle and the cousins. For I don't, grandpa."

"No, dear, we all understand that," said Grandma Elsie soothingly. "We know the monkeys are not the principal attraction for you but merely an additional one."

"Yes, ma'am," returned the child with a relieved sigh. "I don't want anybody to think I don't love Aunt Vi and Uncle Levis and the rest, because I do. But the monkeys are the funniest thing to watch."

"Of course, they are," said her Uncle Herbert. "And who doesn't like fun?"

"I know of no one in this house who objects to it in the right time and place," remarked her father, bestowing a reassuring smile upon the little girl.

"We seem likely to have a merry time while our young naval officer remains in the neighborhood," remarked Mr. Dinsmore.

"Yes, sir," said Edward. "So I understand, and I hope they—the various parties planned—may prove enjoyable."

"I have no doubt they will, my dear," said Zoe.

"I hope they will be in the daytime, so that we children can go," said Lily.

"Even if they do, the monkeys will not be present at all of them," remarked Walter rather gravely.

"But I'm not a monkey, Uncle Walter," she returned in a slightly resentful tone. "You wouldn't have me for your niece if I was."

"No, and you haven't the least look like one. So, if you can do without their companionship, I hope you will be permitted to go to all the parties spoken of."

"If she is a good girl, she shall go to all the parties she's invited to—all the daytime ones in the connection, I mean," said her mother.

"Oh, thank you, mamma!" exclaimed the little girl. "May I go today with you and papa? May I?"

"You shall go somehow and with somebody. We will get it all arranged presently. There are conveyances enough for all to ride if they wish, and it is a delightful day for walking so short a distance if any one prefers to do that."

Some did prefer it, and in a few moments their plans in regard to that were all arranged. In the meantime, Lucilla had made her housekeeping arrangements and dressed for the day. The next-door neighbors had done likewise, and the baby, beautifully attired, was sleeping in her carriage, which Max was proud to draw with his own hands. Thus, they all set out on their trip across the lawn to Woodburn.

They received a joyous welcome there and were told they were just in time to prevent the call from being made in the other direction.

"We were just about to start for Sunnyside," said Violet. "We were all hungry for a sight of my little granddaughter. Is she sleeping?"

"Oh, mamma, she isn't that, and you don't look a bit like a grandmother!" exclaimed Elsie.

"I'm her own grandfather's wife," laughed Violet, "and what's my husband's is mine also. Isn't it, my dear?" turning to him with a pleased little laugh.

"Yes," he replied, "I consider you as having a right to share in all my possessions."

"That's nice and kind of you, papa," said Elsie, "but I don't like my pretty young mamma to be thought old. Folks will surely think so if she is called grandma."

"Well, daughter, I should think a sight of her face would convince anybody of the absurdity of that," the captain said, drawing Elsie to his side and soothing her hair caressingly. Then bending over the babe, who was waking, he said caressingly, "Grandpa's pretty pet! The first grandchild, sweet and beautiful as a lily or a rose."

At that, she looked up into his face and cooed.

"That's a pretty reply to grandpa, baby darling," he said, softly touching her cheek with his lips.

Then she seemed to speak, "I love you, my dear, dear grandpa."

"Oh, that's nice for her to say," cried Elsie, clapping her hands and laughing merrily. "I do believe she does, papa, for see how sweetly she looks at you. Oh, I think she's just the dearest, prettiest baby that ever was made."

"That's rather strong. Isn't it?" laughed Max. "But, I suppose, you are young and have seen comparatively few of her age."

"I really think a brighter or prettier one would be hard to find," said her grandfather.

"And it wouldn't be worth her father's while to pretend to disagree with me," he added, glancing at Max with a twinkle of fun in his eye.

"We are not disposed to contradict you, father," Evelyn said with a smile, "but perhaps it is partly because she is our very own that she looks so pretty to us."

"Oh, there are some of our folks coming up the driveway!" exclaimed Ned. "Why, they are grandma and Uncle Herbert, oh, and Uncle Walter, too, I do believe!"

"And I think you are right," said his father. Then, he hurried forth to meet and welcome the approaching guests. Violet followed closely in his footsteps, the others a little more slowly.

Warm greetings were exchanged, then came a gathering about the carriage. Evelyn and Max were gratified by hearing Walter say he really thought her the prettiest young baby he had ever seen.

"And so far she's as good as she is pretty," said Lucilla, "a bit bairnie to be proud of."

"There's nobody here who will contradict you in that," said Violet, gazing admiringly upon the sweet baby face.

"She seems a fortunate little one. She has come to the right place, I think," remarked Herbert.

"Yes, the right place to be loved and adored," said Violet. "I suppose partly because we have had no baby among us for some years."

"I'm glad we have one now and that she's my little niece—the dearest, prettiest baby in the land!" cried Elsie, bending over the child and regarding her with loving admiration.

"Where's Harold?" asked Violet. "I wonder he didn't come with his mother and brothers."

"He has gone to visit some patients who have been longing for his return," replied Herbert. He added laughingly, "They actually appear to think him a better physician than either Cousin Arthur or myself. I presume he will be in after a little while, though. And yonder, I believe I see grandpa and grandma with Edward and his own lovely little family."

"Ah, that is very well," said the captain, "the more the merrier."

The new arrivals met a hearty welcome, spent a delightful half hour, then returned to Ion. They had scarcely left Woodburn when a servant came to tell the Sunnyside folk that callers were there awaiting the return of its owners.

"Who are they?" asked Max.

"The folks from the Oaks and Beechwood," was the prompt reply.

"Oh, our own connections," said Lucilla. "Father, you, Grandma Elsie, Mamma Vi, and the rest, you will accompany us. Won't you? I think it would be pleasant for us all."

Evelyn and Max added their urgent invitation, and all accepted except Herbert, who excused himself on the plea that there were patients whom he ought to call upon promptly.

Max and his wife and sister found their callers seated upon the veranda at Sunnyside, enjoying a view of the beautiful grounds and chatting cozily together while awaiting their coming.

Cordial greetings were exchanged. The baby was noticed and admired, and someone asked if she could still talk as well as she did yesterday.

"Can't you, my pet?" asked her father, leaning over her.

An answer seemed to come from her lips, "I'll try, papa, if you can help me."

"I really think she can talk now quite as well as she did yesterday," Max said with gravity.

"And I presume she will be able to whenever her father is with her," laughed Violet.

"And when he is gone, perhaps she may succeed when Cousin Ronald is by," said the captain. "I shall certainly not be surprised if she does."

"It probably will not be so very long before she can use her own tongue," said Mr. Lilburn.

"And we will hope she will use it aright as she grows up to girlhood and then to womanhood," returned her grandfather, gazing affectionately upon the little one now nestling safely in her mother's arms.

"Your first grandchild, is it not, sir?" asked Mr. Lilburn, addressing the captain.

"Yes," he replied, "and her coming has given me some serious thoughts about my increasing years. I believe I am growing to an old man."

"Not so very," laughed Cousin Ronald, shaking his head. "I have been a grandfather for years, and when I began the business, I was older than you are now, sir."

"And to me he doesn't seem so very old even yet," Annis said with an affectionate smile.

"That sounds pleasant, coming from the lips of my bonny young wife," Mr. Lilburn said, returning her smile.

There was a momentary silence, then the elderly gentleman went on in a meditative tone, "Life in this world has many blessings and many trials, but the Bible tells us, 'As thy days, so shall thy strength be.' In my experience, that promise has been fulfilled many, many times. Friends, the day after tomorrow is the Sabbath. Suppose we meet together, as we were wont to do in the past, and have 'strength' as the subject for the Bible lesson. I invite you all to come to Beechwood for that very purpose."

"Thank you very kindly, sir," said Captain Raymond, speaking for all. "But, please allow me to offer Woodburn as the place for meeting, it being more central and—so near this—better suited to the entertainment of my little granddaughter, whose parents would hardly like to go leaving her behind."

Cousin Ronald laughed at that. "No, and that would be a bad lesson to begin her education with—the keepin' her oot o' the Bible class. I'm not particular where our class shall meet, and Woodburn will suit me as well as any ither place."

Just then, there were arrivals from Fairview and the Laurels, which caused the subject to be dropped for the time. But it was taken up again after a little, and Woodburn was finally settled upon as the place for the next Sunday's Bible class.

CHAPTER
NINETEENTH

THE FINE WEATHER continued. Sunday was bright and beautiful—the woods bright with autumn tints and the air balmy and sweet with the scent of late fruits and flowers. The Ion, Fairview, Roselands, Beechwood, Woodburn, Sunnyside, and the Laurels people went to church in the morning, and in the afternoon most of them gathered at Woodburn to spend an hour in the study of the Bible, Mr. Ronald Lilburn being the leader of the class.

"Our subject today," he said, "is the strength the Lord promises and gives to His people—His own loved ones, His servants, in the hour of need. 'As thy days, so shall thy strength be.' Captain Raymond, can you bring to our attention any other promise of strength as it is needed?"

"Yes," replied the captain, "here in the fortieth chapter of Isaiah, we read: 'Hast thou not known? Hast thou not heard, that the everlasting God, the Lord, the Creator of the ends of the earth, fainteth not, neither is weary? There is no searching of His understanding. He giveth power to the faint, and to them that have no might He increaseth strength. Even the youths shall faint and be weary, and the young men shall utterly fall: but they that wait upon the Lord shall renew their strength; they shall mount up with wings as eagles; they shall run and not be weary; and they shall walk and not faint.'"

"A most beautiful passage," said Mr. Lilburn, "Now, friends, I think each one of you has one or more passages selected. Please read aloud in turn as you sit without waiting to be called upon."

Violet's turn came next, as she sat beside her husband. She read: "'I will love Thee, O Lord, my strength. The Lord is my rock, and my fortress, and my deliverer; my God, my strength, in whom I will trust; my buckler and the horn of my salvation, and my high tower.'"

Her mother sat next, and she read: "'The Lord God is my strength, and He will make my feet like hinds' feet, and He will make me to walk upon mine high places . . . This day is holy unto the Lord: neither be ye sorry: for the joy of the Lord is your strength.'"

Then Gracie read: "'The king shall joy in thy strength, O Lord; and in my salvation how greatly shall He rejoice.'"

Lucilla then read: "'Unto Thee, O my strength, will I sing: for God is my defense, and the God of my mercy.'"

"'Seek the Lord and His strength: seek His face evermore,'" read little Elsie.

Then Harold: "'I can do all things through Christ who strengtheneth me.'"

Then Herbert: "'Trust ye in the Lord forever; for in the Lord, JEHOVAH, is everlasting strength.'"

Then Max: "'Let him take hold of my strength, that he may make peace with Me; and he shall make peace with Me.'"

Then Evelyn: "'Strengthened with all might, according to His glorious power, unto all patience and long suffering with joyfulness.'"

The others said their selected texts had been read. There was a moment's pause, and Mr. Lilburn said, "I think it altogether likely that every one present who has gone past the meridian of life could tell of personal experience of the fulfillment to her or himself of that gracious, precious promise, 'As thy days, so shall thy strength be,' and I, for one, should be very glad to hear their testimony to our Heavenly Father's faithfulness to His promise.

A moment's silence reigned, then the captain said, "And you, Cousin Ronald, being the eldest and chosen leader, might well be the first with your story of the Lord's goodness to you and His great faithfulness to His promise."

"I am entirely willing," the old gentleman returned pleasantly. "The Lord has been exceedingly good to me through all the years of my life. I have had very many troubles, trials, and difficulties, but His grace and the many great and precious promises of His Word have helped me through them all. I have seen the grave close over wife, children, parents, and friends, but I have been sustained under that sore trial by the glad hope of meeting them all in that better land where there is no more death, no sin, no parting—where all is righteousness and peace and joy forevermore.

"And even in this world, the Lord has given me much to repair my losses and renew the joys of my younger days," he added with a loving look and smile directed to Annis.

She returned the smile and spoke in low, pleasing tones, "I, too, have had some sore trials and can testify to the Lord's faithfulness to His promise, 'As thy days, so shall thy strength be.' Years ago my heart was torn with grief over the deaths of parents, brothers, sisters, and other dear ones. There have been other trials also, but the Lord's promise has never failed. He has brought me safely through them all and is making my later days my best days—full of peace, comfort, and happiness."

It was now Mrs. Elsie Travilla's turn, as she sat next to her Cousin Annis. She spoke in low, sweet tones, distinctly audible in the quiet of the room, "I give my testimony to the Lord's faithfulness to that gracious promise, 'As thy days, so shall thy strength be.' I never knew a mother's love and care, for mine died when I had been but a few days in this world. My father was so far away that it seemed much as if I had none. But I was in the care of those who taught me of Jesus and His love as soon as I could understand the meaning of the words. While yet a very little child, I learned to know and love Him. I loved my home, too, and it was a sore trial to be brought away from it. Then, when I first saw my father and perceived that he did not care for me, my heart was almost broken and only the love of Jesus helped me to bear it.

"That trial was soon happily over, but later in life sore bereavement came, as my nearest and dearest were called away from earth. But even then, strength was given me according to my days, and while grieving for myself, I rejoice heartily for them. And these later days are, oh, so full of peace and joy and love!"

Harold sat near his mother, and he was next to speak. "I have as yet seen no very great trials, save the loss of my father. But in going into the recent war with Spain, I felt that I was risking life and limb, but the Lord sustained me with the thought that I was doing so for the sake of oppressed and suffering fellow-creatures and with that thought came strength according to my days there."

"And my experience was much the same as Harold's," added Herbert.

"Mine also," said Max. "When we went into the fight at Manila, I feared wounds and death, but I knew we were in the right—fighting to free the downtrodden and sorely oppressed. Knowing that the Lord had the disposal of it all, I had strength given me according to my days there. Now you, dearest," he added in an undertone to his wife.

Eva said in low, gentle tones, "I have seen sorrow, losing my dearly loved father before I had grown to womanhood, but my strength was according to my day, the Lord comforting me with His love. And as a wife and now a mother, having a kind, new father, and brothers, sisters, and friends, I am now a very happy woman indeed."

A slight pause, then Captain Raymond spoke.

"I have had many, many blessings and some trials also. My dear father died when I was a young lad, and my own mother died when I had scarcely more than reached man's estate. My brother and sisters had gone from this earth also, and I was left alone with small means but good health. I was still quite a young man when I met a sweet young girl who had been, like myself, bereft of all her nearest relatives. We loved, married, but I had to leave her often, sometimes for long intervals, for the duties of my profession. We were very happy when together, but in a few years she left this world for a better land and the three children God had given us to my sole care, though I had to be away most of the time upon the sea. I have since found another to share my life with—one as dear and loving as Grace had been," he added with a look and smile directed to Violet that thrilled her heart with joy and love.

It was her turn now, and she began at once, "I have had a peaceful, happy life, both as a young girl and as a married woman. Some deep sorrows did come to me years ago—first the death of a darling younger sister, Lily, and then that of the best and dearest father that ever lived." Her voice trembled with emotion, but she went on. "But then in those sad hours was fulfilled to me that precious promise, 'As thy days, so shall thy strength be.' Though I feel it to be only reasonable to expect other and greater trials in the future, I can trust my Heavenly Father to fulfill it to me again and again until I, too, reach that blessed land where there is no more sin or sorrow or suffering."

No one else in the room made any lengthened response to the invitation to tell of the fulfillment to them of the gracious promise, "As thy days, so shall thy strength be." Each one merely commented that they believed in it and trusted in it for their future but did not share openly with the others at that time how that promise had as of yet been fulfilled in each of their lives.

Then Violet went to her organ. She played a short prelude and began to sing a hymn, in which they all joined her:

"In every condition, in sickness, in health,
In poverty's vale, or abounding in wealth,
At home or abroad, on the land, on the sea,
As thy days may demand
shall thy strength ever be."

CHAPTER TWENTIETH

THE WHOLE CONNECTION seemed filled with a desire to entertain their returned travelers, especially Max, whose present stay among them would be but short. And that the baby might accompany her parents, the gathering together of the relatives and friends was always in the afternoon.

On Monday, they took dinner and spent the afternoon at the Laurels, on Tuesday at the Oaks, Wednesday at Roselands, and Thursday at Beechwood. There the younger ones had great sport, Cousin Ronald and Max helping them.

They were all on the veranda after dinner, chatting pleasantly among themselves, when Ned exclaimed, "Oh, let's have some fun on the lawn! We may play there. Mayn't we, Cousin Ronald?"

"You may, Cousin Ned," answered the elderly gentleman with a pleased smile, "and mayhap I'll tak' a turn wi' ye, if I'm not deemed sae auld as to spoil the sport."

"Oh, I think it would be fun for us to have you with us, sir!" cried Ned. "Now, how many of you boys and girls would like to join in a game of 'I spy'?"

In reply to that query, all the children present immediately expressed a desire to take part in the game, and they promptly adjourned to the grounds. All were familiar with the game.

"Now who shall be the one to hide his eyes?" asked Ned, his look and tone of voice showing a desire to fill the position himself.

That was evident to the others, and two or three of the cousins said at once, "You, Ned. You'll do as well as any other."

So, the base being chosen, Ned covered his eyes, and the others scattered and hid behind bushes, trees, and summerhouses. Then from every direction came the cry, "All ready!" Ned's eyes were instantly uncovered, and away he ran, looking about him searchingly from side to side.

Presently catching a glimpse of a familiar coat worn by his cousin Eric Leland, "I spy Eric Leland!" he shouted. "I'll beat you in to base," he cried, then turned and ran back to the chosen base—the lower step of the front veranda.

Both boys ran as fast as their young legs could carry them, but Ned reached the base and Eric became "It."

Directly after these two came running from their spots, so did all the others engaged in the game. Just as the last one had reached the goal, there came a very angry growl, quite apparently from under the veranda.

"How dare you rude youngsters come tramping and stamping here in this rude way? It's enough to kill a man with a headache like mine, and I won't stand it. Clear out, every one of you."

For a moment or two, the children seemed quite thunderstruck. Then they began asking each other in awed, frightened tones, "Who is it? And where is he? Is there a room for him under there? And will he come out and fight us?"

Then all at once Ned, Elsie, and the cousins from the Oaks and Fairview began to laugh.

"Oh, it's Cousin Ronald or Max, and we needn't be a bit afraid," they said.

But at that the voice spoke again, "I, a relation of yours? You think I'd own any o' you for relations o' mine?"

"Yes, I do think so," replied Ned stoutly. "I know you're either Cousin Ronald or Brother Max, and whichever you are, I'm not a bit afraid of you, because you're both as good and kind as ever you can be."

"That's the way to talk," replied the voice. "You are a pretty good boy, I perceive. So go on with your play, and if you don't make a racket here and hurt my head, I'll not interfere with you."

"Where is your head, cousin or brother, whichever you are?" asked Ned.

"On my shoulders, saucebox," was the reply.

At that all the children laughed.

"That's funny," said Ned. "Mine is at the top of my neck."

"Well, keep it there," said the voice. "Now run off to your play, all o' ye, and leave me in peace to nurse my head and get rid of the ache."

"Yes," said Ned, "but first I'm going to look for Cousin Ronald and Brother Max, because I'd like to know which has been trying to cheat us and pretend to scold."

He straightened himself and looked earnestly along the veranda as he spoke. Evidently, the company there had been listening to what was going on and enjoying the sport, Cousin Ronald and Max among them. Captain Raymond was there, too, standing at the top of the steps and looking as if he had been having a share of the fun.

"You are having a great deal of fun. Aren't you, my young friends?" he asked. "To hear and see it all makes me rather hungry for a share of it. Would you object to my joining you?"

"Oh, no! No, indeed!" cried several young voices. "Please come. We'll be glad to have you."

So the captain stepped down and joined them.

That started the older people. Not only Mr. Lilburn and Max hastened to join the players, but Chester and Lucilla, Dr. Harold and Gracie, Dr. Herbert, and Dr. Arthur Conly.

They all seemed to renew their youth, entering heartily into the sport to the great delight of the children, the two ventriloquists increasing it by the use of their peculiar talent. Sometimes the players were surprised and puzzled by voices, unlike any of theirs, calling from different quarters, but presently the more knowing ones would give a merry shout that would open the eyes of the others to the fact that it was only a ventriloquial trick for their amusement.

When they grew tired of "I spy" other games were tried with success, and it was only as the time for going home drew near that they ceased their sport and rejoined the older members of the party upon the veranda.

Evelyn was sitting there with her baby on her knee, and many of the children gathered about her, saying they wanted a bit of fun with her—the baby—before going home. They all wanted to hear her talk.

"But she is too young to talk," said Evelyn. "She will hardly be able to say anything for months and months to come."

"Oh, her father can make her talk," laughed Eric. "If he tells her to, she'll mind him. Won't you, little baby dear?"

"Yes, I will. Babies ought to do what their papas tell them to."

The words seemed to come from the little lips, and the children turned to see if Max was near. He was, and he smiled in response to each of their questioning glances.

"Doesn't she do pretty well for so young a talker?" he asked.

"Yes, sir, with her father to help her," laughed Eric. "But I'm afraid she won't be able to do so well when you are away on shipboard. Unless Cousin Ronald is somewhere near by," he added, as an afterthought to his comment.

"Yes, I like Cousin Ronald," the baby voice seemed to say.

"And you love your aunties. Don't you?" asked Elsie Raymond, leaning over her.

"Yes, I love you and all the other ones."

"And don't you love your cousin doctor, who takes care of you and mamma when you need him?" asked Dr. Harold, joining the group.

"Yes, indeed! Will you be my uncle some day?"

"I hope so," laughed Harold. "You will make a nice little niece, I think."

"And I think he will be a nice uncle," laughed Gracie, who was standing by his side.

Captain Raymond, too, was near, the baby being as attractive to him as to any one else—except, perhaps, her parents.

"I should like to be able to prove that very soon," said Harold with a significant glance at the captain.

At that, Gracie blushed and gave her father a loving, entreating look that seemed to say, "Don't be angry with us, father dear. I love you, and we are not rebellious."

"'Patient waiting is no loss,'" he said with kindly look and smile. "I love my daughter too well to be in a hurry to give her away."

"What will you do when your papa goes away to his ship, baby?" asked Eric.

"Stay at home with mamma," was the reply, at which the children all laughed.

But now, the carriages were at the door, and they must hasten to prepare for their homeward drive.

It was but a short one from Beechwood to Woodburn, and to that hospitable home went not only the immediate family, but the Sunnyside folk and Grandma Elsie and her two sons, Harold and Herbert.

An inviting tea was ready for them on their arrival, and after it, they had a delightful social evening together, music and conversation making the time pass very swiftly.

But the guests were all disposed to retire to their homes at a reasonably early hour. First, however, they sang a hymn together. Then the captain read a portion of Scripture and led them in a prayer full of love and gratitude for the numberless blessings that sweetened their lives. Then the goodnights were said, and the outsiders departed to their homes. But there was no sadness in the partings for all fully expected to meet again in a few hours.

When Gracie came to her father for the usual goodnight caress, he took her in his arms and held her close. "My own darling daughter," he said low and tenderly, "you don't know how dear, how very dear you are to your father. Millions could not buy you from me."

"Dear, dear papa, it is very sweet to have you love me so," she responded in tones trembling with emotion, "and I think my love for you is as great as yours for me."

"Yet you want me to give you away?"

"No, sir, only to take another son as a partner in the concern when you think the right time has come," she answered, smiling up into his face.

At that, he gave her a smiling caress.

"So I will when I think that time has come," he said, "but till then I hope you can be happy in my home, under my care, and loved as one of my God-given children."

"I am sure I can, papa, and I shall never, never be willing to go too far away to see and talk with you every day."

"That is pleasant for me to hear," he said, "and I hope to keep you in this home with me even after you exchange your name for another. If you and Harold grow tired of that, I think I can find room on this estate for another dwelling not inferior to Sunnyside, put it up, and furnish it for my second daughter, who is not to be treated with any less favor than her elder sister and brother."

"Oh, papa, how good you are to me!" she exclaimed low and feelingly. "I am so glad and thankful that I was born your child. But I should love to be that even if you were poor and couldn't do anything for me."

"I believe you would, my darling," he returned. "But now bid me goodnight and go. For it is time you were resting after all the excitement and fatigue of the day."

"Yes, papa, dear, dear papa," she said, putting her arms around his neck and kissing him with ardent affection. "You are so kind to me, and, oh, how I do love you! I wouldn't marry even Harold, whom I dearly love, if I knew that he would take me far away from you."

"Nor could I be willing to give you to him if that was to be the result. But there seems little or no danger of that, as his home and near connections are in this neighborhood, and he seems to have no desire to leave it. My greatest objection to the match is the mixture of relationships it will bring about. You, my own daughter, will be my sister-in-law, and Harold son-in-law to his sister. Still, as there is no blood relationship between you two and you seem so devotedly attached to each other, I have not felt that I had any right to forbid the match."

"Yes, papa, and you were very, very kind not to do so, for dearly as I love Harold, I would never marry him without your consent."

"No, I know you would not, my darling, for I have not a more obedient, bidable child than you. But I must not keep you longer from your needed night's rest."

Then, laying his right hand gently upon her head, he gave her the fatherly blessing Lucilla loved so well: "The Lord bless thee and keep thee; the Lord make His face shine upon thee, and be gracious unto thee; the Lord lift up His countenance upon thee and give thee peace."

"Dear papa, thank you," she said with emotion and glad tears in her eyes. "I do love that blessing, and I hope you will have it as well as I."

"I hope so, daughter," he said. "Nothing could be better for either of us, and I am exceedingly glad that he who has won your young heart is a Christian man."

CHAPTER
TWENTY-FIRST

MAX AND EVELYN were home at Sunnyside, leaning over their sleeping babe, their faces shining with love and joy.

"The darling!" exclaimed Max, speaking low and tenderly. "She seems to me the dearest, loveliest child that ever was made."

"To me, too," returned Eva with a low and sweet laugh, "though I know that is because she is yours and mine. There must have been very many others quite as beautiful and sweet."

"Yes, no doubt, and I suppose it is because she is our very own that she seems so wonderfully attractive and lovable to me. And yet she seems to be so to others not related to her."

"Quite true, Max, and my heart sings for joy over her, yet we cannot tell that she will always be an unmixed blessing, for we do not know what her character in future life may be. Oh, Max, we must try to train her aright, and we must pray constantly for God's blessing upon our efforts, for without His blessing they will avail nothing."

"No, dearest, I am sure of that, and my darling daughter will be always remembered in my prayers. That will be almost all I can do for her in that line, as my profession will call me almost constantly to a distance from home. You, dearest, will have to bear the burden of both training and education, except such parts as money can procure."

"I know, I know," Evelyn replied in moved tones, "and you must pray for me that I may have wisdom, grace, and strength according to my day."

"That I will, dear wife. We will converse each day by letter. Shall we not?"

"Yes, indeed, and you shall know as well as written words can tell you how baby grows, and looks, and learns. And she shall know her papa by seeing his photograph and hearing a great deal about him from mamma's lips."

"It is pleasant to think of that," Max said with a smile. "And of my homecoming, which I hope will be rather frequent, as we are at peace and I am likely to be on some vessel near the shore of this, our own land."

"Oh, I hope so!" exclaimed Evelyn. "How I shall look and long for your coming! Ah, how I do envy those women whose husbands are always at home with them."

"Oh, my dear, some of them would be glad if they weren't. Unfortunately, all marriages are not the happy one that ours is. Some husbands and wives have little love for each other and little enjoyment in each other's society."

"Alas, my dear, that is a sad truth," sighed Evelyn sadly. "Our mutual love and happiness in each other is still another cause for great gratitude to God for our blessings."

"Yes, indeed, and I thank Him every day—and many times a day—for the dear, lovable wife He has given me."

"As I do for my best and dearest of husbands," she said in response.

"And oh, what a number of dear relatives and friends our marriage has given me! Friends they were before, but not really relatives. I am so glad to be able to call your father, sisters, and little brother mine. It is so sad to have no near relatives."

"Yes, I feel it must be, though I have not known it by experience, having always had my dear father and sisters, Lu and Gracie. But now, dearest, it grows late, and you are looking weary. Had you not better get to bed as quickly as possible?"

"Yes, my dear, thoughtful husband. It has been quite an exciting day, and I am weary," she said, turning from the cradle to him, her eyes shining with love and joy.

ℵ ℵ ℵ ℵ ℵ

After Gracie had said goodnight and retired to her own apartments, the captain and Violet sat chatting together in the library for some time. It was quite past their usual hour for retiring, when at length they went up to their bedroom. The door was open between it and the next room, which had formerly been occupied by Gracie but was now given up to Ned, as he had graduated from the nursery much to his own gratification. He considered it plain proof that he was no longer a baby boy, but a big fellow hastening on toward manhood.

"I have been feeling somewhat anxious about our little boy," Violet said in an undertone to her husband, while laying aside her jewelry. "He was so flushed and excited while getting ready for bed. Oh, hark, how he is talking now!"

She paused in her employment and stood listening, the captain doing likewise.

"I got to the base first, and it's your turn to be 'It,' Eric!" Ned called out in excited tones.

Tears started to Violet's eyes as she quickly turned toward her husband with a questioning, appealing look.

"I fear he is indeed not well," returned the captain, moving toward the open door. "We will see what can be done for him."

Violet followed. The captain lit the gas, and both went to the bedside. Ned was rolling and tumbling about the bed, muttering and occasionally calling out a few words in regard to the game he imagined himself playing.

"Ned, my son," the captain said in soothing tones, "you are not at play now, but at home in bed. Try to lie still and sleep quietly."

The captain took the little hot hand in his as he spoke. He was surprised and alarmed at its heat and that the little fellow did not seem to know where he was or who it was that spoke to him.

"Oh, Levis, the child is certainly very ill," said Violet in low, trembling tones. "Would it not be well to telephone for one of my brothers? I am sure either of them would come promptly and cheerfully if they knew our boy was ill and we wanted advice for him."

"I haven't a doubt of it, dearest, and I will go at once to the telephone," replied the captain, leaving the room, while Violet leaned over her little son, smoothing the bedclothes and doing all she could to make him more comfortable.

At Ion, most of the family had retired to rest, but Harold had lingered over some correspondence in the library, and he was now going quietly up the stairway when he heard the telephone bell. He went directly to the instrument, saying to himself a trifle regretfully, "Somebody wanting the doctor, I suppose. Hello!" he called and was instantly answered in Captain Raymond's unmistakable voice.

"I am glad it is you, Harold, for we want you badly, as soon as you can come to us. Ned is, I fear, very ill. He has a high fever and is quite delirious."

"I will come at once," returned Harold. "Poor, dear, little chap! His uncle loves him too well to let him suffer a moment's illness that he may possibly be able to relieve."

As Harold turned from the instrument, his mother's bedroom door opened, and she stood there arrayed in a dressing gown thrown hastily over her nightdress.

"What is it, Harold, my son?" she asked. "I heard the telephone. Are any of our dear ones ill?"

"Don't be troubled, mother dear," he returned in tenderly respectful tones. "It was only a call from Woodburn to say that little Ned is not well, and that they would like me to come and do what I can for him."

"And you are going?"

"Yes, mother, with all haste."

"I should like to go with you to do what I can for the child and to comfort poor Vi."

"Oh, don't, mother! Please go back to your bed, take all the rest and sleep that you can, and go to them tomorrow. That is your eldest doctor son's prescription for you. Please, won't you take that advice?" putting his arm about her and kissing her tenderly.

"Yes," she said, returning the caress with a rather sad sort of smile, "for I think he is a good doctor, as well as one of the best of sons." And with that, she went back to her bed, while he hurried away to the patient.

It was an anxious night to both him and Ned's parents, and the morning brought little, if any, relief to them or the young sufferer.

Chester and his wife were breakfasting cozily together that morning when Captain Raymond walked in upon them unannounced.

"Father!" cried Lucilla, springing up and running to him. "Good morning. I'm so glad to see you. But—oh, father, what is the matter? You look ill."

As she spoke, she held up her face for the usual morning kiss.

He gave it with affection and said in moved tones, "Your little brother is very, very ill. Harold and we have been up with him all night. He is no better yet, but we do not give up hope."

"Oh, I am so sorry!" she sighed, tears filling her eyes. "He is such a dear, little fellow and has always been so healthy that I have hardly thought of sickness in connection with him."

Chester had left his seat at the table and was standing with them now.

"Do not despair, captain," he said with feeling. "All is not lost that is in danger, and we will all pray for his recovery if consistent with the Lord's will."

"Yes, the effectual, fervent prayer of the righteous man availeth much, and the Lord will spare our dear one if He sees it is for the best," returned the captain feelingly.

"Father dear, you look so weary," Lucilla said with emotion. "Let me do something for you. Won't you sit down to the table and have a cup of coffee, if nothing else?"

"Thank you, daughter. Perhaps it would help to strengthen me for the day's trials and duties," he replied, accepting the offered seat.

They were about to leave the table when Max came in.

"Good morning, father, sister, and brother," he said, looking about upon them with a grave, concerned air. "I have just heard bad news from one of the servants — that my little brother is very ill. Father, I hope it is not true?"

"I am sorry, Max, my son, to have to say that it is only too true," groaned the captain. "We have been up with him all night, and he is a very sick child."

"Oh, that is sad indeed! Can I help with the nursing, father, or be of service in any way?"

"I don't know, but come over all of you as usual to cheer us with your presence and perhaps make yourselves useful in some other way."

"Thank you, sir. I shall be glad to do anything I can to help or comfort, but, if our baby should cry, might it not disturb poor little Ned?"

"I think not. We have him in the old nursery. Her cry, if she should indulge in one, would hardly reach him there. Even if it did, he is not in a state to notice it. So come over as usual. The very sight of you will do us all good."

"I was going in to town as usual," said Chester, "but if I can be if any use —"

"Your help will not be needed with so many others, and you can cheer us with your presence after you get home in the afternoon," returned the captain in kindly, appreciative tones. "Are Eva and the baby well, Max?" he asked, turning to his son.

"Quite well, thank you, father, and you will probably see us all at Woodburn in an hour or so."

With that, Chester and the captain departed.

At Ion, Mrs. Elsie Travilla came down to the breakfast table evidently attired for a drive or walk. No one was surprised, for the news of Ned Raymond's serious illness had already gone through the house, causing sorrow and anxiety to the whole family.

Herbert, too, was ready for a drive, and presently after leaving the table, he took his mother over to Woodburn in his gig. Dr. Conley also arrived about the same time, having been telephoned to in regard to the illness of his young relative.

Several days followed that were sad ones to not only the immediate Woodburn and Sunnyside families, to whom little Ned was so near and dear, but to the other more distant relatives and friends. All of them were ready and anxious to do anything and everything in their power for the relief of the young sufferer and to comfort and help the grieved and anxious parents.

But Harold's skill and knowledge of the disease and the most potent and effectual remedies did more than all other human means to remove it and restore the young lad to health. Harold was at length able to pronounce his young patient free from disease and on a fair road to entire recovery of health. Violet embraced her brother and wept for joy, while the father and sisters—the older brother also—were scarcely less glad and thankful.

"Come into the library, Harold, and let us have a little private chat," the captain said in tones husky with emotion.

For some moments they sat in silence, the captain evidently too much moved to command his voice in speech. But at length, he spoke in trembling and low tones.

"Harold, dear fellow, I can never thank you enough for saving the life of my little son. You were the instrument in the hands of God our Heavenly Father. Money cannot pay the debt, but I should like to give a liberal fee as my expression of the gratitude felt by us all, especially your Sister Violet and myself."

There was emotion in Harold's voice also as he answered, "My dear brother, don't forget that it was not so much your son as my own dear little nephew I was working to save. Thank you heartily for your desire to reward me with a liberal fee, but I feel I can well afford to use all the knowledge, strength, and skill I possess for the benefit of my dear ones without any payment in 'filthy lucre.' But, my dear brother, there is one great reward you could give me which I should be far from despising—which I should value more than a mint of money, or any amount of stocks, bonds, or estate."

He paused, and after a moment's silence, the captain spoke, "You mean Gracie? Surely you forget that I long ago consented to the match."

"If I would serve for her as Jacob did for Rachel, but I want her now. And if you will give her to me directly, I will watch over her with all the care and solicitude of both a devoted husband and physician. I think you will find that marriage will not break down her health. Has her health only improved under my care and may we not hope to see still greater improvement when she is my dear devoted wife? For she does love me, unworthy as I am."

The captain sat for a moment apparently in deep thought. Then he said, "Being of the medical profession, you ought to know better than I what will be likely or unlikely to injure her health. I believe you to be thoroughly honest and true, Harold, and if such is your opinion and you are willing to live here in this house for at least the first year and afterward in one that I shall build for you and her on this estate, you may have her in a few months. You know, she will want a little time for the preparation of her trousseau," he added with a smile.

"Thank you, captain, thank you with all my heart!" exclaimed Harold, his face aglow with obvious happiness.

At that moment, Gracie's voice was heard speaking to some one in the hall without.

The captain stepped to the door and opened it.

"Gracie, daughter," he said, "come here for a moment. Harold and I have something to say to you, dear."

She came immediately, blushing and smiling with a look half of inquiry and half of pleased expectation on her sweet and lovely face.

Her father, still standing by the door, closed it after her, took her hand, drew her into his arms, and kissed her tenderly and fondly.

"My child, my own dear child," he said, "I have given you away or promised to do so as soon as you can make your preparations and—when you—want me to give up my right in you to another."

"Oh, no, papa, not that," she returned, her eyes filling with tears. "Papa, am I not your very own daughter? And shall I not always be so, as long as we both live?"

"Yes, yes, indeed, my own precious darling, and this is to be your home still for at least a year after — you drop my name for Harold's."

"I shall never drop it, father, only add to it," she returned with both tears and smiles.

Harold stood close beside them now.

"And you are willing to share mine, dearest. Are you not?" he asked, taking her hand in his.

"Yes, indeed, since I have your dear love," she answered low and feelingly.

"And I think he has been the means of saving your dear life and now your little brother's also," her father said with feeling. "So I cannot refuse you to him any longer, my darling, sorrowful thing as it is to me to give you up."

"Oh, don't give me up, dear father, don't!" she entreated with pleading look and tone. "Surely, I shall not be less yours because I become his also."

"No, my dear child, I shall surely be as much your father as ever. Shall I not, Harold?"

"Surely, sir, and mine also, if you will accept me as your son."

Violet came to the door at that moment.

"May I come in?" she asked. "Or would that be intruding upon a private interview?"

"Come in, my dear. We will be glad to have you," replied her husband.

She stepped in and was a little surprised to find the three already there standing in a group together.

It was Harold who explained.

"Congratulate me, sister. I have obtained leave to claim my bride as soon as she can make ready for the important step."

"Ah? Oh, I am glad, for you richly deserve it for what you have done for our precious little Ned."

"Thank you, sister," Harold said with emotion, "but give God the praise. I could have done nothing had He not blessed the means used."

"True, and my heart is full of gratitude to Him." Then, turning to Gracie, "I am very, very glad for Harold to be, and feel that he is, rewarded, but, oh, how shall I ever do without you—the dearest of dear girls?"

"I have not yet consented to her departure from her father's house," said the captain, turning a proud, fond look upon his daughter. "I have stipulated that we are to have them here in this house for at least a year and then in another to be built upon this estate—if they wish to leave us."

"Oh, I like that!" exclaimed Violet. "It removes all objections—except with the regard to the mixture of relations," she added with a slight laugh. "But I am forgetting my errand. Ned is awake and asking hungrily for his father and his doctor."

"Then we must go to him at once," said both gentlemen promptly.

Gracie added, "And I, too, if I may, for surely he would not object to seeing his sister also."

"No, indeed," said Violet, "and the sight of your dear, sweet face, Gracie, could not, I am sure, do anything but good to any one who sees it."

"Ah, mamma, I fear you are becoming quite a flatterer," laughed Gracie. "But it must be for father or the doctor to decide my course of conduct on this occasion."

"You may come, if you will promise not to say more than a dozen unexciting words to my little patient," Harold said in a tone half way between jest and earnest.

"I promise," laughed Gracie. "It seems I have to begin to obey you now."

"I think you began a year or two ago," he returned laughingly. "You have been a very satisfactory patient."

"I am glad to hear it," she said. "Father, have I your permission to go with you to take a peep at my little brother?"

"Yes, daughter, if you will be careful to follow the doctor's directions."

"I will, father, first following in his and your footsteps," she said, doing so along with Violet, as the two gentlemen, having moved into the hall, now began mounting the broad stairway.

They found the young patient lying among his pillows, looking pale and weak. His eyes shone with pleasure at the sight of them.

"I'm glad you've all come," he said feebly. "I want a kiss, mamma."

She gave it and bent over him, softly smoothing his hair. "Mother's darling, little man," she said in trembling tones, pressing kisses on his forehead.

"There, Vi dear, that will do," the doctor said gently. "Let the rest of us have our turn. Are you quite easy and comfortable, Ned, my boy?" laying a finger on his pulse as he spoke.

"Yes, uncle. Give me a kiss and then let papa and Gracie do it, too."

"Be very quiet and good, my son. Do just as uncle tells you, and you will soon be well, I think," the captain said in cheery tones when he had given the asked-for caress.

Then Gracie took her turn, saying, "My dear little brother, get well now as fast as you can."

Then the doctor banished them all from the room, bidding them leave him to his care and that of the old mammy who had again and again proved herself a capital nurse in the family connection.

CHAPTER
TWENTY-SECOND

CAPTAIN RAYMOND, VIOLET, and Gracie now returned to the library, where they found Lucilla at the typewriter answering some letters for her father.

"Oh, you have all been up to see Neddie. Haven't you?" she asked, judging so by the expression of their faces.

"Yes, daughter," replied the captain, "but the doctor would allow only an exceedingly short call. So much depending upon it, we must all be careful to follow his directions."

"Yes, indeed, the dear, little brother!" she exclaimed with emotion. "But surely something pleasant has happened to you, Gracie dear, for you are looking very happy."

"As I am and ought to be," returned Gracie, blushing vividly. "Father and the—and others, too—have been so kind to me."

"Oh, father means to reward Harold. Does he?" laughed Lucilla. "Well, sister dear, if you like it, I am glad for you."

"Your father has, indeed, been very kind to our pair of lovers," said Violet, smiling upon both her husband and Gracie, "and the best of it is that he has stipulated that they are to stay here with us for the first year of their married life."

"After that to remain on the estate but in a separate house if they wish it," added the captain.

"Oh, how nice!" cried Lucilla. "Harold really does deserve it."

"As does Gracie also," said their father, "for she has been sweetly submissive to her father's will."

"It would have been strange if I had been anything else toward such a dear, kind father as mine," she said, regarding him with an expression of ardent affection, which he returned, smiling fondly upon her.

The door opened, and Max stood upon the threshold of the room.

"Am I intruding?" he asked, pausing there.

"No, my son. We wish to have no family secret from you. Come in and join us," replied his father, and Max stepped in, closing the door behind him.

"You are looking happy," he said, glancing about upon them with a pleased smile. "And it is no wonder. It is such good news that our dear, little Ned is convalescing."

"Yes," said Lucilla, "and I think Gracie here is somewhat rejoiced over Harold's promised reward for his excellent services."

"Ah, I suppose I know what that is," said Max, glancing at the blushing and smiling face of his younger sister. "You are to be 'It' this time. Aren't you, Gracie?"

Her only reply was a low, sweet laugh, but their father answered, "Yes, I have withdrawn my objection to a speedy union, as I felt that Harold deserved a great reward, and he preferred that to any other."

"And when is it to be?" asked Max.

"When she has had ample time to prepare her trousseau, Max."

"And I fear that will take so long that I shall miss the sight," sighed Max.

"Don't despair, son. You and I may be able to get an extension of your leave of absence," said his father hopefully.

"Perhaps, father, if they do not delay too long."

"But we could hardly have a grand wedding now while Neddie is so ill," said Violet, "especially as Harold is his physician. And we want Max here at the wedding and don't want Harold to leave our dear, little boy till he is fairly on the road to recovery. Now, how shall we manage it all?"

"Perhaps your mother might be of help in the arrangements," suggested Lucilla.

"Perhaps Harold would want to tell her himself of — the change of plans," said the captain.

At that moment, the door opened, and mother and son appeared on the threshold, both looking very cheery and bright.

The captain sprang to his feet and hastened to bring forward an easy chair, while Violet exclaimed, "Oh, mother, I am so glad you have joined us! I was just on the point of going to ask you to do so."

"I suppose to tell me the good news I have just heard from Harold," was the smiling rejoinder. "But he was the one to tell it, daughter. And captain," turning to him, "I thank you for the change in your decision in regard to a most important matter, which Harold feels to be a great reward for what he has been enabled to do for our dear, little boy."

"I am glad I had it in my power to do something to show my appreciation for his invaluable help," the captain said with evident emotion.

"Where is Eva?" exclaimed Lucilla. "She should be here with us on this important occasion."

"Yes, she is one of the family," assented Captain Raymond heartily. "I will go and bring her," said Max, hurrying from the room to return in a minute with his wife by his side and his baby in his arms.

The little one was cooing and smiling.

"Excuse me, friends and relatives, for bringing in this uninvited young girl, for I can assure you she will not repeat anything that is said," laughed Max, as Eva took possession of a chair handed her by Harold, and he gave the child to her. The door opened again at that moment, and Elsie Raymond's voice was heard asking, "May I come in, papa?"

"Yes, daughter, you are wanted here," was the pleasant-toned reply, and as she came near to him, he drew her to his knee, saying, "We are all talking of Gracie's wedding, trying to decide when it shall be."

"Oh, is it going to be soon, papa?" she exclaimed. "I thought it wasn't to be for years yet. And I don't want my Gracie to be taken away from us yet to another home."

"No, and she shall not be for a year or more and then not out of the grounds."

"Oh, I am glad of that! You will build them a house on our grounds. Will you, papa?"

"I hope to do so," he said. "But now you may listen quietly to what others are saying. Mother," turning to Mrs. Travilla, "I think we can hardly yet set the exact date for the ceremony that will give you a daughter and me a son. We will want our little Ned to be well enough to enjoy the occasion and to spare his doctor for a wedding trip of more or less length."

"Yes, sir, I agree with you in that. Perhaps Christmas Eve would be a suitable time for the ceremony. Neddie will probably be well enough by then to be present, and if the bride and groom want to take a trip, Herbert and Arthur Conly can give any attention or prescriptions needed during Harold's absence."

"Don't forget, mother, that it is the groom's privilege to fix the month," said Violet. "And, Harold," turning to him, "please don't let it be so early as Christmas, because I want Gracie here then. It would hardly seem like Christmas without her."

"Well, then, how would New Year's Day do for the ceremony?" suggested Lucilla.

"Much better than Christmas, I think," said Violet.

"So I think," said the captain. "They are both too soon to suit my desires, but—I guess I have already relinquished them."

"It would be the best New Year's gift you could possibly bestow upon me, captain," said Harold.

"What is your feeling about it, my dearest?" he asked in an undertone, tenderly bending over Gracie as he spoke.

"If you are suited, I am satisfied," she returned in the same low key and with a charming smile up into his eyes.

"I, for one, like the New Year's gift idea," said Evelyn. "Gracie to give herself to Harold as such, and he himself to her as the same."

"Yes, it is a pretty idea," assented Grandma Elsie. "But, as Vi has reminded us, it is Harold's privilege to set the month, but Gracie's to choose the day."

"New Year's would suit me better than any later day, but I want my ladylove to make the choice to suit herself," Harold said, giving Gracie a look of ardent admiration and affection.

"I like Eva's idea," she said with a blush and smile. "So am more than willing to say New Year's day, if that suits you, Harold, and, of course, if—if dear, little Ned is well enough by that time to attend and enjoy the scene."

"I think he will be," said Harold, "at all events, if we have the ceremony performed here in the house."

"I should prefer to have it here than anywhere else," said Gracie with gentle decision.

"I, too," said Harold.

"Let it be understood that such is to be the arrangement," said the captain. "In the meantime, Gracie, daughter, you can be busied with your shopping and overseeing the dressmakers."

"Thank you, father dear," she said. "But I have an abundance of handsome wearing apparel now, and I shall not need to get anything new but the wedding dress."

"Nonsense!" exclaimed Violet, "you must have a handsome traveling dress and loads of other nice things. As soon as Neddie is well enough to be left by us for some hours, we must go to the city and do the necessary shopping."

"Yes," added the captain, "remember that your father wants you to have all that heart could wish for your trousseau, if—if he is handing you over to another rather against his will."

"I trust I shall never give you cause to regret it, sir," said Harold pleasantly. "But I must go now to my young patient," he added, rising to his feet. "Adieu for the present, friends. I know that you can arrange any and all remaining matters without my valuable assistance."

With that, he left the room, and the talk between the others went on.

Harold was pleased to find his young patient sleeping quietly. The improvement in his condition was steady from that time, so that in another week, it was deemed altogether right and wise to begin preparations for the approaching nuptials.

Relieved from anxiety about Ned and supplied by the captain with abundant means, the ladies thoroughly enjoyed the necessary shopping. Daily, they brought home an array of beautiful things for the adornment of the bride that was to be. At the same time, Max returned to his vessel but with the promise of a short leave of absence to enable him to attend the wedding. That made it easier to part with his wife and baby for the time.

Here we leave our friends for the present, preparations for the wedding going merrily on. The lovers were very happy in each other and the bright prospect before them. The captain was not very discontented with the turn events had taken, and Grandma Elsie was full of quiet satisfaction in the thought of Harold's happiness and that she herself was to have so sweet a new daughter added to her store of such treasures.

The End

Invite little Elsie Dinsmore™ Doll Over to Play!

Breezy Point Treasures' Elsie Dinsmore™ Doll
brings Martha Finley's character to life in this
collectible eighteen-inch all-vinyl play doll
produced in conjunction with
Lloyd Middleton Dolls.

The Elsie Dinsmore™ Doll comes complete
with authentic Antebellum clothing and a
miniature Bible. This series of books emphasizes
traditional family values so your and your child's
character will be enriched as have
millions since the 1800's.

Doll available from:

Breezy Point Treasures, Inc.
124 Kingsland Road
Hayneville, GA 31036 USA

Call for details on ordering:

1-888-487-3777

or visit our website at
www.elsiedinsmore.com